A GIR

Rose met the handsome Dutch surgeon,
Werdmer ter Sane, quite by chance,
but she could hardly refuse when he
asked her to help nurse his little
godson. But what she didn't understand
was *why* he had asked her—as he
seemed to dislike her so much . . .

A GIRL NAMED ROSE

BY

BETTY NEELS

MILLS & BOON LIMITED
15–16 BROOK'S MEWS
LONDON W1A 1DR

First published in Great Britain 1986
by Mills & Boon Limited

© Betty Neels 1986

Australian copyright 1986
Philippine copyright 1986
This edition 1986

ISBN 0 263 75337 9

Set in Monophoto Plantin 10 on 11 pt.
01–0486 – 55998

Made and printed in Great Britain by
Richard Clay (The Chaucer Press) Ltd,
Bungay, Suffolk

CHAPTER ONE

THE early summer sky, so vividly blue until now, was rapidly being swallowed up by black clouds, turning the water of the narrow canal to a steely grey and draining the colour from the old gabled houses on either side of it. The two girls on the narrow arched bridge spanning the water glanced up from the map they were studying and frowned at the darkening sky. The taller of the two had a pretty face, framed by dark curly hair, her blue eyes wide with apprehension; the smaller of the two, with unassuming features, straight pale brown hair piled into a too severe topknot and a pair of fine brown eyes, merely looked annoyed.

'It's going to rain,' she observed, stating the obvious as the first slow, heavy drops began to fall. 'Shall we go back if we can, go on, or find shelter?' She added in a matter-of-fact way, 'I haven't the faintest idea where we are.' She began to fold the map, already wet, but before she had done so the rain came down in earnest, soaking them in moments. Worse, there was a sudden flash of lightning and a great rumble of thunder.

The pretty girl gave a scared yelp. 'Rose, what shall we do? I'm soaked.'

Her companion took her arm and hurried her off the bridge. 'I'll knock on a door,' she said, 'perhaps there's a porch . . .'

The brick road they were on was narrow and the houses lining it were solid seventeenth and eighteenth-century town mansions built by wealthy Dutch merchants, their doors massive, their windows

5

symmetrical, presenting an ageless calm in this backwater of Amsterdam, and not one of them had a porch. A second flash of lightning sent the smaller girl up the steps of the nearest house, to bang resoundingly on the great brass door knocker.

'You can't,' objected her companion; she didn't answer, only knocked again.

The door opened and she found herself staring into an elderly bewhiskered face; it belonged to a stout man, almost bald except for a fringe of hair with a stern expression and pale blue eyes. She swallowed and drew a breath.

'Please may we stand in your doorway?' she began. 'We're wet and lost.'

Before the man could answer a door behind him opened and shut and a voice asked, 'English, and lost?' and said something in Dutch so that the man opened the door wider and stood aside for them to go in.

The hall they entered was very impressive; its black-and-white tiled floor partly covered with thin silky rugs, its white plastered walls hung with paintings in heavy frames; the man who stood in its centre was impressive too, well over six feet tall, with great shoulders and the good looks to turn any girl's head. Any age between thirty and forty, Rose guessed, wondering if his fair hair was actually silver.

She hung back a little; this was the kind of situation Sadie could cope with admirably; her pretty face and charming smile had smoothed her path through three years of training at the children's hospital where they both worked; they could certainly turn things to her own advantage now.

'Come in, come in.' The blue eyes studied them sleepily. 'Very wet, aren't you? Give your cardigans to

Hans, he'll get them dried for you and come into the sitting-room while I explain where you are.'

He smiled at them both, but his eyes lingered on Sadie's glowing face, damp with rain, her curls no less attractive for being wet, whereas Rose's hair hung in damp tendrils, doing nothing to aid her looks.

He held out a large hand and shook their proffered ones firmly. 'Sybren Werdmer ter Sane,' he said briskly. It was Sadie who answered him. 'I'm Sadie Gordon and this is Rose Comely.' She smiled bewitchingly at him as he opened a big double door and ushered them into the room beyond.

It was a large lofty apartment, its ceiling was plaster with pendant bosses, and a central recessed oval with a border of fruit and flowers. The windows were large and draped with heavy swathes of plum-coloured velvet, and the same rich colour predominated in the needlework carpets strewn on the polished wood floor. The furniture was a thoughtful mixture of the old and the new. Vast display cupboards flanked the steel fireplace with its rococo chimney-piece and mirror, a pair of magnificent seventeenth-century armchairs, elaborately carved and velvet-cushioned, stood on either side of a small table inlaid with mother-of-pearl. A pair of William and Mary winged settees were on either side of the fireplace and there were a number of lamp tables and small comfortable easy chairs.

A delightful room, Rose thought, but Sadie said at once, 'I say, what a simply heavenly room—you'd never guess from the outside . . .'

'Er—no, I suppose not. Do sit down; I've asked Hans to bring you some tea and in the meantime tell me how I can help you.'

'Oh, Rose will explain; we're hopelessly lost—my fault, I wouldn't stop to look at the map.'

'Where are you staying?'

Rose answered him in her quiet sensible voice. 'At a small hotel called "De Zwaan", it's close to the Amstel Hotel, down a narrow side street. We got here yesterday, quite late in the evening, and we're leaving again in the morning. We're on a package tour; six of us, but the other four didn't want to explore. We were all right to start with, but these small streets are all alike, aren't they? Besides, they are so picturesque we just walked on and on . . .'

'It is so very easy to get lost!' commented their host. 'But you aren't too far out of your way. Will your friends worry?'

'They went shopping and they won't be back at the hotel until the shops close. We have a kind of high tea at half past six.'

'Ah yes, of course,' murmured Mijnheer Werdmer ter Sane; he had never eaten high tea in his life and indeed was a little vague as to what it was, but there was no need for him to comment further for Sadie, who had been frankly staring around her, wanted to know if the large painting of a family group wearing the stiff clothes of a couple of hundred years earlier were any relation to him. He led her over to take a closer look and when Hans came in a few minutes later with the tea tray, paused only long enough to ask Rose to pour out. 'What is it you say in England? "Be Mother".'

She poured the tea from a silver teapot into paper-thin china cups, reflecting that no one had ever called her motherly before; homely, plump, dull, un-interesting—all these, repeated so often that they no longer hurt; indeed anything her stepmother said to her now had no effect at all, and even though she was aware that there was truth in what she said, she enjoyed the friendship of a large number of people who didn't seem to notice her unassuming looks. The others sat down presently and she handed cups and as she did so admired her host's good manners, and when he turned to her and asked her what she thought of Holland, she answered him unselfconsciously in her pleasant voice. After a few moments she noticed that he was asking apparently casual questions, all of which she answered with polite vagueness, completely wasted from her point of view for Sadie broke in to give him chapter and verse about St Bride's, with a wealth of unnecessary detail about their training and how they had passed their exams not six months previously and now held Staff Nurses' posts. 'Rose is the gold medallist,' she informed him, 'she's the only one of us with any brains; anyway she studied and we didn't. There were always other things to do in the evenings when we were off duty.' She added ingenuously, 'You know, housemen and the senior medical students.'

Mijnheer Werdmer ter Sane's blue eyes rested fleetingly on Rose's face; what he saw there caused him to say kindly, 'I imagine that a gold medal is worth at least half a dozen housemen, your family must be very proud of you.'

This tactful remark didn't have the effect he expected; Rose's face flooded with colour and then went pale and she mumbled something, luckily lost in Sadie's chatter. 'That's why we're here,' she explained, 'we've been saving up for months to have a holiday— to celebrate, you know. Only a week.' She sighed dramatically. 'Back to work in two days' time.'

She turned blue eyes to him. 'You speak perfect English. Have you been in England?'

His voice was smooth. 'Yes, from time to time. We

are, of course, taught it in school; Dutch is a difficult language so we need to be proficient in the more widely used tongues.'

'You sound like a professor,' declared Sadie.

'Oh, I do hope not. Now shall I explain your street map to you?'

A nicely worded hint that they should think of leaving; Rose got to her feet at once and followed him to the table between the windows and handed him her map, and he took a pen from his pocket, marked a cross on it and then inked in their return route. 'So that you will know exactly where you had got to,' he pointed out, 'but I hope you will allow me to drive you back to your hotel—there's always the chance that you will get lost again.' He handed Rose the map and tugged an embroidered bell-rope by the fireplace and when Hans came, spoke to him in his own language.

Hans came back almost at once with their cardigans and their host said easily, 'It's a bare ten minutes drive; Hans will fetch the car round.'

He helped Sadie into her cardigan and answered her light-hearted chatter good naturedly and then turned to Rose. But she was already buttoned neatly into hers, standing quietly with the map in her hand.

'We are very grateful,' she told him gravely. 'It's quite frightening, being lost—and then the storm . . . but there's no need for you to drive us back, now we know how to follow the map we can walk quite easily.'

'I am sure that you could, you seem to be, if you will forgive me for saying so, a very practical young lady, but I should prefer to take you back; besides I have enjoyed the company of both of you—the gratitude should be mine for helping me to pass a dull afternoon in my own company.'

Oh, very polished, thought Rose, even if he doesn't mean a word of it.

They went out into the hall and before Hans opened the front door, she had time to have another quick look round. The staircase was at the back of the hall, thickly carpeted, with barley sugar balusters, curving up gracefully to the floor above; there was a massive chandelier above their heads and a great carved oak table against one wall. It was tantalising to have a glimpse of such a fine house before they were out on the narrow pavement and being ushered into the dignified dark grey Rolls-Royce motor car standing there.

Sadie slid into the front seat, exclaiming prettily that it had always been her ambition to travel in a Rolls, and Rose got into the back, quite content to do so, only half listening to her friend rattling on about one thing and another while she looked out of the window, trying to see both sides at once; she wasn't likely to come to Amsterdam again for some time, indeed if ever, and she wanted to see as much as could be crowded into their brief stay.

At their hotel they bade their host goodbye, thanked him once more, and Sadie said, 'I hope you come to London and we see you again; don't forget where we are—St Bride's.' She gave him a beguiling smile as they shook hands. 'I think you'd be much more fun to go out with than any of the housemen I know!'

He made some laughing reply and opened the hotel door for them.

Inside Rose said doubtfully, 'Sadie, weren't you a bit—you know...? After all he is a complete stranger...'

Sadie laughed. 'Look who is talking—who knocked on his door, then?'

'Well, we had to get in out of the rain and I didn't know he was living there, did I?' They began to climb the steep stairs to their rooms on the top floor. 'The others will be back and I'm famished.'

The rest of the party were milling around the small, plainly furnished rooms gossiping about their day. As Rose and Sadie reached the top landing they surged out of doors, full of questions.

'Where have you been?' demanded a lanky girl with a long face. 'We've been getting worried; after all, Rose, you've got all the plans for tomorrow and the money for the hotel . . .'

Rose began mildly and was cut short by Sadie's exuberant voice. 'We walked miles and got lost and then there was that awful storm so Rose knocked on the door of a simply huge house and we had tea there and came back in a Rolls-Royce.'

The lanky girl goggled at her. 'You're making it up.'

'It's quite true,' said Rose composedly. 'We did get lost, Alice. Did you have a good time shopping?'

'I'll say,' a girl with red hair interpolated, 'a good thing you've got the money to pay the bill here, Rose, I'm skint.'

'I'll pay this evening, we don't leave until after lunch, so if there's any money over we'll share it out.'

The little group dispersed to tidy for the evening and Rose went into her own room and changed her damp dress for a cotton jersey and did her hair again. Which done she made up her face and then stood peering into the very small looking-glass which hung on the wall. She was undoubtedly a plain girl; not, she conceded, hopelessly so, her skin was good, she had nice eyebrows and her eyes were passable, only her nose was too short and turned up very slightly and her mouth was too wide, and as for her hair . . . fine and silky reaching to her waist but most uninterestingly pale brown. She pinned it severely to the top of her head and went to join the others. There was no point in her being sorry for herself and indeed she seldom was, but today it had struck her forcibly that no man, certainly not one as handsome as Mijnheer Werdmer ter Sane, would bother to look at her twice. Not that he had ignored her; his manners had been beautiful but she thought that they would have been just as beautiful if she had been an elderly aunt or a chance acquaintance he wasn't likely to see again.

They trooped down to their high tea and joined the other members of the coach party in the basement dining-room; they were mostly elderly couples with a sprinkling of middle-aged ladies on their own who treated the six of them with a guarded friendliness and greeted them now with looks of mild reproof.

'We spent a delightful afternoon doing the canal trip,' one of the single middle-aged ladies told them. 'It's something you shouldn't have missed. Most instructive.' She began to enumerate the various sights they had seen, and they, making formidable inroads into the cold meat and ham on the table, murmured and muttered in reply.

'And what did you do?' asked a cosy matron kindly.

'Went to the shops—they are super.' Alice took another slice of bread and buttered it lavishly. 'But Rose and Sadie went for a walk and got caught in the storm. They came back in a Rolls-Royce . . .'

Sadie looked daggers at her but Rose answered composedly enough, 'Yes, we were lucky enough to be offered shelter by someone who kindly drove us back here.'

'But you didn't know him?' one of the single ladies, a wispy faded blonde, asked with faint excitement.

'Not then, we didn't,' explained Rose in her sensible way, 'but we do now. We were lost you see and had to take shelter.'

An old man with glasses pronounced it his opinion, that foreign parts, while interesting, were unreliable. A remark which closed the conversation for the simple reason that it was difficult to answer.

They weren't to leave until directly after lunch on the following day and since there was enough money over after Rose had paid their bill, the six of them voted to take a trip along the city's canals. They prudently packed their bags before going to their beds; there would be ample time in the morning for sight-seeing, but much as they had enjoyed their brief stay they had no wish to be left behind with almost no money in their pockets.

They got themselves up early, had the coffee and rolls and cheese the hotel provided and made a brisk beeline for the Central Station from which the boats left.

There weren't too many people about at nine o'clock in the morning; they got on to one of the first boats to leave and settled down to enjoy themselves.

It was a splendid morning and the old houses, viewed from the water, looked at their very best. They viewed the smallest house in the city, the Munt, and the patrician houses lining the canals, with suitable interest while the guide, switching from English to German to French with enviable ease, pointed out the highlights of the trip. They were back again soon after ten o'clock and trooped down Damrak to the Dam Square, intent on coffee before they went back to the hotel. They were waiting to cross the square, thick with traffic and noisy little trams when Sadie caught Rose by the arm.

'Look,' she cried loudly. 'There he is, over there . . .'

Too far away for him to see them, Rose judged, watching the Rolls slide between two trams with Mijnheer Werdmer ter Sane at the wheel. Besides, what would be the point, even if he did? They weren't going to meet again.

They lunched at the hotel, cheese rolls and coffee because the hotel didn't cater for cooked meals at midday, and then they boarded their coach. Rose felt a twinge of regret as they were driven through the city's heart and its suburbs; streets of neat houses and flats, all exactly alike and not in the least resembling the lovely old houses in the centre of the city. At least she had investigated the inside of one of them, and very nice it was too. She allowed her thoughts to dwell on the pleasures of living in such a house, lapped around with comfort, no, not comfort, luxury. She said out loud, 'I wonder if he was married?'

Sadie, sitting beside her, chuckled. 'Well, of course he would be—I daresay he had a handful of children too, on the top floor with Nanny.'

Rose was surprised to find that the idea quite upset her.

The coach kept to the motorway, giving her little time to do more than glimpse the villages to be seen on either side of it. 'Next time I come, if I ever do,' she told Sadie, 'I shan't go on a single motorway; I'm sure there is heaps to see.'

'Well, I don't suppose you'll come again,' said Sadie comfortably; she sounded faintly smug; more or less engaged to a solid young man with his feet firmly on the first rung of banking, her own future was already cut out for her. She added, 'I mean, you are sure to get offered a sister's post—there's Sister Coutts on children's medical due to retire, and the junior night sister leaving to get married at Christmas.'

Rose resolutely brushed away the vague daydreams floating around inside her head. She didn't much care for medical nursing and nor did she like night duty; she would like to work on the children's surgical ward, but chance was a fine thing; the ward sister there was young enough to be there for another twenty years, and certainly had no intention of marrying. Rose consoled herself with the thought that she might be going there as a staff nurse. Perhaps when she had more experience she would look for a sister's post at another hospital, as far away from her home as possible. Not that it was home any more. Even after two years it hurt to think of her father; they had lived so happily together after her mother died until quite out of the blue, just after she had started training, he had told her that he was going to marry again.

Her stepmother was still quite young, a well preserved forty, with a pretty face and a charm which she lavished on Rose when there was anyone there to see it. They had disliked each other on sight, but Rose had done her best to understand her father's re-marriage and had tried hard to like her stepmother. It wasn't until her father died suddenly and her stepmother married again within six months of his death, that Rose admitted to herself that she didn't like her and never would. She couldn't stand Mr Fletcher, a tall thin man, who doted on her stepmother but treated Rose with cold severity. It was like having two strangers in her home and during the following year she had gradually stopped spending her days off and holidays there, feeling an interloper each time she went to the village near Tunbridge Wells. Instead she had answered her mother's elder sister's invitation to visit her and now she felt more at home there in Northamptonshire. Her aunt lived at Ashby St Ledgers, in a comfortable little house, a rather sterner version of Rose's mother, but kind and affectionate and ready to welcome her niece. She was an enthusiastic gardener, a staunch supporter of the church and had a finger in every village pie and was looked after by a little dumpling of a woman Rose remembered from her childhood when she had been taken on a visit to Aunt Millicent. Both ladies, in their way, made much of her, her aunt in an off-hand manner which didn't quite conceal her very real affection, and Maggie with a cosy warmth made apparent by the nourishing meals she dished up and the hot milk she insisted Rose should take to bed each night.

'I'd like to see more flesh on your bones,' she would mutter, pressing the nourishing drink into Rose's hands when she went to bed, and each time Rose went to stay, she would return with a large cake in her case; devoured with gratitude by Rose and her friends the moment it was unpacked.

She thought of her aunt now; she would be going to see her in a few weeks' time but first she would have to settle down on whichever ward she was sent to. Hopefully back on children's surgical, she had been there for three months as a student nurse and loved it. She turned to say something to Sadie but that young lady was asleep, her pretty mouth slightly open, her curls, rather untidy now, framing her charming face. No wonder the Dutchman had been so taken with her, thought Rose, quite without envy.

The bus stopped just before they reached Zeebrugge and they all got out and had tea and a biscuit; the tea—a teabag in a saucer with a glass of almost boiling water, and no milk, was refreshing but not at all like the dark strong brew they shared in each other's rooms when they came off duty. They were off again within fifteen minutes and shortly after went on board, where they left everything in the bus and climbed the stairs to the upper decks. They knew the journey would take four hours and there was still the drive to London from Dover; they wouldn't be at the hospital until midnight at least. Luckily none of them were on duty until one o'clock the next day. Their main thoughts were now centred on food. Lunch had been light and hours ago; Rose counted what was left of the money and then shared it out between the six of them. There wasn't a great deal, not enough to go to the restaurant with the other travellers in the coach, but there was a cafeteria on board. They trooped along its counter, getting value for their money, spending it on rolls and butter, cheese, hard-boiled eggs and cups of tea.

It had been great, they all agreed, sitting round a table, munching, for the most part the food had been good and generous; they had seen a lot and their fellow passengers had been friendly.

'But next time I go,' declared Sadie, 'I'll travel by car and eat all the time at those heavenly restaurants we saw and never went into. I'd like to spend at least a week in Amsterdam, wouldn't you, Rose?'

Rose drank the last of her tea. 'Oh, yes—but I'd like to see a lot more of Holland too. But Amsterdam was smashing.'

Alice said slyly: 'I bet you'd like to meet that Dutchman again . . .'

'Yes I would.' Rose spoke readily enough in her composed way. 'One meets someone and wonders about them and that's as far as it goes. Shall we go on deck for a bit? We'll have to sit in that coach presently.'

It was most fortunate that the coach went within a hundred yards of St Bride's and the driver, being a kind man, took them almost to the door. They tumbled out, exchanging goodbyes with the other passengers, collected their cases, thanked the driver, handed him the tip Rose had been jealously guarding, and hurried across the street from the hospital to the Nurses' home. The warden on duty let them in with a good deal of shushing and requests to be quiet, and rather dampened in spirits, they went softly up the stairs to the second floor where the staff nurses had their rooms. They did not linger over getting ready for bed; there was a brisk to-ing and fro-ing in competition for baths, quick good nights and then sleep. Rose, laying her head in a cloud of soft brown hair on her pillow, spared a thought for the Dutchman and then resolutely shut him out of her mind. The last few years had taught her to make the best of things and try to improve on them if possible, and never, never, to waste time on wanting something she couldn't have: to see him again. She closed her eyes and slept.

There wasn't much leisure in the morning; they got up for breakfast for the simple reason that if they didn't they would be hungry, but it was a cheerful rather noisy meal, for everyone wanted to know about their trip. Besides there was the hospital gossip to catch up on, and once they were back in their rooms, there was the unpacking to do, clean caps to make up and another pot of tea, made in their own little pantry, and by then it was time to go to the office, one by one, to be told where they were to go on duty.

There were no surprises for Rose; staff nurse on

children's surgical and she was to report to Sister
Cummins at one o'clock. As an afterthought she was
asked if she had enjoyed her holiday, to which she
made a suitable reply before getting herself tidily out
of her superior's presence.

Sister Cummins seemed pleased to see her; she was
a big, vigorous young woman, quite wrapped up in her
work and a splendid nurse. She had no use for nurses
who weren't prepared to work as hard as she did, and
made a point of saying so, so that she wasn't popular,
but Rose got on well with her, going calmly about her
work and refusing to take umbrage at some of Sister
Cummins' more caustic remarks. And as for the
children, they got on splendidly together; she settled
down quickly into the chaotic routine of the ward, and
if, just now and again, her thoughts turned to the
lovely old house and its handsome owner in
Amsterdam, she shook them off briskly.

The ward was very busy, for the hospital did a good
deal of major surgery in the paediatric wing; very
small patients with heart conditions, cystic hygroma
which had become infected and needed surgical
treatment, pyloric stenosis, club feet, hydrocephalus.
Rose, trotting quietly to and fro between the cots, had
her heart wrung a dozen times a day and yet her days
had their lighter moments too. The convalescent
children, full of good spirits, were as naughty as she
could wish and Sister Cummins, once they were on
the road to recovery, didn't believe in checking them
more than was necessary. There was a play-room
where they were taken each day under the care of two
of the nurses and they screamed and shouted and
played together and more often than not, fell asleep.
Rose never had much time to spend in the play-room,
there were so many ill children to nurse, but it pleased

her to hear the normal racket even if it did give her a headache by the end of a busy day.

She was to have a long weekend in a week's time; the two weeks she had already done on the ward had flown and although she had had days off she hadn't gone away. She hadn't heard from her stepmother but she hadn't expected to, she sensed that she wouldn't be welcome if she went to her home. Besides, there was nothing for her there any more. It would be nice to see Aunt Millicent and Maggie again; she would help in the garden and take her aunt's old dog, Shep, for gentle walks and eat huge meals.

It had been more than a full day; three operations and a street accident. Rose, going off duty over an hour late, looked as tired as she felt. A long hot bath, and never mind supper, she decided, she could make tea for herself and there were some biscuits in the tin and perhaps if one of her friends felt like it she would nip down the street to the fish and chip shop and get a bag of chips.

Head well down, she ran down the wide stone staircase leading to the front hall; there wasn't anyone about; those who had an evening off had gone long ago, those on duty were busy seeing to suppers, hurrying to be ready in time for the visitors in half an hour. She jumped the last two steps and ran full tilt into the man standing at the foot of the stairs.

She had butted him in the waistcoat and her head shot up. Not, for heaven's sake, one of the consultants. It wasn't, it was the Dutchman, quite unshaken, smiling down at her.

'Well, well,' he said pleasantly, 'Nurse Comely, literally bumping into me.'

She blushed, hating herself for doing so, unaware that the colour in her cheeks made her almost pretty.

She said nervously: 'Oh, hullo, Mijnheer Werdmer ter Sane. What a surprise. Have you come to visit someone?'

He was smiling a little. 'Yes, are you going off duty?'

It was silly of her heart to leap so violently, and even sillier that she had thought even for a split second that he was going to ask her to spend the evening with him. She must be mad. She said soberly, 'Yes, I am. Very late. We're busy today.' She added succinctly: 'Children, you know.'

'Ah, yes.' He stood for a moment, not speaking, and she saw that he wanted to go but didn't want to be too abrupt about it.

'Well, I must hurry,' she told him brightly. 'I'm supposed to be going out.' She held out a hand. 'It was nice to see you again, goodbye.'

He shook her hand gently and said just as gently, 'Indeed, a pleasant surprise for me, too, Nurse.'

She gave him a quick smile and crossed the hall very fast and went out of the door to cross the road to the nurses' home. Now if she had been Sadie she would have managed better; turned on the charm, made some amusing remarks . . . only she wasn't Sadie. She went to her room and not allowing herself to brood, undressed, lay in the bath until impatient thumps on the door got her out of it, drank her tea in the company of such of her friends as were off duty too, and went to bed early, pleading a headache.

She wasn't allowed peace and quiet for long. Sadie, coming off duty a couple of hours later, burst into her room with an excited, 'Rose, Rose, wake up, do. He's here—our Dutchman, I've just met him in the hall and guess what, he's a surgeon and knows old Cresswell'—Mr Cresswell was the senior consultant at the hospital,

an elderly grumpy man who somehow became a
magician once he had a scalpel in his hand—'I asked
him why he was here.'

'You didn't,' expostulated Rose in horror.

'I did. Why not? And he said I'd know soon
enough. What do you suppose he wants?'

Rose sat up in bed and hugged her knees. 'Sadie, I
don't know. Probably to consult with someone, or give
a lecture or borrow something.'

'He remembered me,' said Sadie, ignoring this
remark. 'He said, "Ah, my charming visitor." He told
me he was delighted to see me again. I hope he's here
in the morning. He might ask us out to lunch or a
drink or something.'

Rose eyed her friend soberly. 'You perhaps, not me,
and anyway, it might not be quite the thing; he's much
more likely to have lunch with old Cresswell and the
other consultants.'

Sadie grinned at her. 'The trouble with you, Rosie,
is that you have no romance in you, not one ounce.'

Rose curled up in bed. 'Well, let me know what
happens. We'll both be at first dinner tomorrow.'

It was half way through the morning when Sister
Cummins came down the ward to where she was
bending over one of the cots, adjusting an intravenous
drip. 'Staff, will you go to the office? Now. Miss
Timms wants to see you.'

'Me, heavens, whatever have I done?'

'Your guess is as good as mine. I'll take over here.
Leave your apron in my office and tidy your hair.'

Two minutes later Rose, hair smoothed beneath her
muslin cap, went as fast as she dared without actually
running through the labyrinth of passages to the
centre of the hospital where Miss Timms had her
office, tucked away behind an outer office, guarded by

her two assistants. There was another door to her office too, opening directly on to the passage Rose was racing along. As she reached it she skidded to a halt. Miss Timms had a loud voice. 'I'm sorry that I must disappoint you, Mijnheer Werdmer ter Sane, Nurse Gordon is a very good nurse and I agree with you that she has a pleasant manner, but she isn't very skilled in the nursing of children and toddlers. Now Nurse Comely is our gold medallist and is at present staffing on the acute children's ward; she has already spent some months there during her training and is absolutely trustworthy and highly skilled.'

Rose was standing like a statue; quite forgetful that it was a most reprehensible thing to eavesdrop; moreover, listeners never heard good of themselves, a fact borne out by the Dutchman's remark. His voice wasn't as loud as Miss Timms', but it was deep and very clear; she didn't miss a syllable.

'Then I must bow to your good advice,' he was saying. 'I am sure that if you recommend her so highly, Nurse Comely will suit the case very well. But it seemed to me that she lacks a certain light-heartedness—she is a very quiet girl, is she not?'

Miss Timms didn't answer at once, and Rose held her breath and beat down her sudden rage. Quiet was she, lacking in light-heartedness, was she? Why didn't he go all the way and say that she was plain?

'Not a girl that one would notice,' pursued Mijnheer Werdmer ter Sane blandly, 'but of course she will spend a good deal of time with her patient. You see, Miss Timms, I had hoped for someone who would be able to cheer up the child's mother—distract her thoughts and so on, and it seemed to me that Miss Gordon filled the bill.'

Rose ground her splendid little teeth and let out a

breath as he went on, 'But I bow to your wisdom—if I
might have a few words with her?'

'She should be here by now.' Miss Timms' voice
held a faint triumph at getting her own way. It also
sent Rose soft-footed past the door, to tap on the outer
office and be admitted, to be urged into Miss Timms'
office without more ado.

After living for several years with her stepmother,
she had learnt to hide her feelings. She was slightly
pale and she was breathing rather fast but that could
be put down to her sudden summons. She said
politely, 'Good morning, Miss Timms, you wanted to
see me?' and then, 'Good morning, Sir,' in a colourless
voice. Her glance was so quick that she didn't see his
sudden sharp look which was perhaps a good thing.

CHAPTER TWO

MISS TIMMS said, 'Ah, Staff Nurse Comely,' in a voice which suggested that she was about to pronounce judgment on Rose's head. 'I must explain why I have sent for you.'

Rose sat, inwardly seething. She looked the picture of composure with her pretty hands folded tidily on her lap and her dark eyes upon Miss Timms' face. Mijnheer Werdmer ter Sane sat down too, to one side and a little behind her, very relaxed in his chair although he was watching her from under hooded lids. He still watched her as Miss Timms began to speak in her most impressive voice.

'Mijnheer Werdmer ter Sane is a surgeon, a friend and colleague of Mr Cresswell and he has come to me with a request which Mr Cresswell begs me to grant.' She paused, inflated her massive bosom with a deep, dramatic breath, then went on. 'Doctor ter Brandt, who lives in The Hague, is a friend of both Mr Cresswell and Mijnheer Werdmer ter Sane. He is married to an Englishwoman, a trained nurse from St Athud's, they have a two-year-old son and Mrs ... she glanced at the man sitting quietly listening and said coyly, 'I suppose one calls her Mevrouw?'

'It would be quite suitable if you were to refer to her as Mrs, indeed I would suggest that you address me as Mister.'

Miss Timms bowed her head in majestic acknowledgement. 'Thank you. As I was saying, Mrs ter Brandt is expecting her second child within a few weeks and is

26

therefore unable to deal with the painful situation which has arisen.' She paused again and if her listeners were impatient they gave no sign.

'Two days ago the little boy fell and before his mother could pick him up, had rolled down stone steps leading to the garden. He has sustained a depressed fractured skull and is in the children's hospital in Amsterdam where Mr Werdmer ter Sane is a consultant. His mother is most anxious that he should have an English nurse since she is unable to do much for him herself. Mr Werdmer ter Sane got in touch with Mr Cresswell who kindly suggested that a nurse from St Bride's might be borrowed. I have recommended you for the case, Staff Nurse, you will leave this afternoon. That will be all.'

Not quite all, however. Mr Werdmer ter Sane got to his feet and observed blandly, 'Perhaps I might ask Nurse Comely if she will accept. She may not wish to take the case although I hope that she will.'

She looked at him then. 'Yes, of course, I'll come,' she told him without fuss. She added silently, even though I'm quiet and not light-hearted and not pretty either. She added out loud this time, 'If you are sure that there isn't a nurse who would suit you better?'

His eyes were suddenly intent on hers. He said smoothly, 'If Miss Timms recommends you so highly, I feel sure that the matter is entirely satisfactory. Would you be able to leave at three o'clock this afternoon? We can go by hovercraft from Dover and be in Amsterdam late this evening.'

He glanced at Miss Timms. 'That could be arranged, Miss Timms?'

'Certainly, Staff Nurse may go off duty now and pack what she will need.' She nodded at Rose. 'Very well, Staff Nurse, you may go. Have you enough money to tide you over?'

'No,' said Rose baldly. 'Payday is next week.'

'As I am aware. Come to the outer office in an hour's time and you will receive an advance in cash.'

'Thank you, Miss Timms.' Rose turned to the door and found it being opened for her; her thanks were wooden.

It was well past eleven o'clock; she sped back to the ward, gave Sister Cummins a brief resumé of her interview, listened with sympathy to that lady's opinion of foreigners who came borrowing the best nurses in the hospital without so much as a by-your-leave and was bidden to have her coffee before she left the ward. 'I'll have mine too,' said Sister Cummins gloomily, 'and just whisk through the routine—how far had you got? I suppose I'll be sent some feather-brained idiot . . . I could strangle that man.'

She thumped the coffee-pot down on her desk as there was a tap on the door and called 'come in' in a grudging voice.

Mr Werdmer ter Sane came in, completely at ease. 'Sister Cummins? I've come to apologise for taking your staff nurse away. Believe me, only the urgency of the situation drives me to such a drastic step.' He shot a glance at Rose's calm face. 'I dare say Nurse Comely has already explained to you . . .'

Sister Cummins' wrath was oozing away under his charm. 'Well, it is most inconvenient but I can see that it is urgent.' She waved him to the padded office chair in a corner that no one ever had time to sit in. 'Have some coffee while you tell me about it . . .'

Rose fetched another mug and poured the coffee as he eased himself into the chair and began his explanations; much more succinctly than Miss Timms had done and in half the time. He drank his coffee with every sign of enjoyment too, although by now it was lukewarm and tasted frightful. 'And if I might take up a few more minutes of your time? It would be useful to explain to Nurse Comely what she should bring with her.'

He glanced across at Rose; he looked kind and impersonal. 'Your passport, money, uniform, for you will be at the hospital for some time, I imagine, and whatever you wear out of uniform. Enough for three or four weeks, but I'm sure that if you forget anything Christina ter Brandt will see to it.'

He got up and smiled charmingly at Sister Cummins who smiled back, quite won over. When he had gone she turned to Rose, collecting mugs and putting them on the tray. 'You know, I quite envy you—he is really rather nice. We could do with a few like him in this place.' As Rose reached the door, she added, 'You'd better get cracking, you don't want to keep him waiting.' Just for a moment she looked wistful. 'I wouldn't mind being in your shoes. Bye.'

Rose balanced the tray, kicked the door open with one foot and said, 'I hope I'll come back here. Sister. I'm happy on this ward. I don't suppose I'll be gone for more than a few weeks at the outside.'

She had half an hour before her dinner time; she went to her room, got her case from the depths of the wardrobe and started to pack. Uniform and caps, tights and undies, dressing-gown and slippers and a cotton skirt and a handful of tops as well as a plain linen dress, sandals, make-up and a sponge bag and her rain coat. It was time by then to go to the office and collect her money; most of her month's salary so at least she wouldn't be penniless. She put the envelope in her pocket and went along to the canteen, collected her shepherd's pie, potatoes and beans, and bore her plate to the table where her friends were already sitting.

Sadie greeted her excitedly. 'I say, Rosie, I saw him again coming out of the office—he seemed in a hurry, but he waved. I wonder why he's here.'

Rose speared some pie and added mustard. 'Well,' she said slowly, 'he's here to borrow a nurse—a friend of his with an English wife; their small son has got a fractured skull, I don't know any details, I suppose I'll get those later . . .'

'Later? What on earth do you mean?' She had the attention of the whole table now.

'He's borrowed me. Mind you, he didn't want me particularly, only Miss Timms seemed to think I'd do. It's for a week or two and I'm going at three o'clock this afternoon. Back to Amsterdam.'

'Rose, how absolutely marvellous. And you'll see him every day.'

'I don't know about that, Sadie, I'm going to look after a toddler, not accompany Mr Werdmer ter Sane to nightclubs.'

There was a little burst of laughter and then a spate of questions between gobbling their dinners with one eye on the clock. Milk pudding and strong tea brought their meal to an end and they got up to go back on duty. Only Sadie lingered. 'Have fun, Rose, I wish it was me . . .'

Rose smiled at her friend. 'I'm sure he wishes it was you, too, love. But Miss Timms didn't give him a chance.'

Sadie brightened. 'Keep reminding him about me,' she urged. 'I know I'm going to marry and settle down but I wouldn't mind one final fling.'

Rose finished her packing, showered and got into a cotton jersey shirtwaister; not high fashion, but very simple and suitable for a journey, then she went to phone her aunt.

Aunt Millicent took the news calmly, merely hoping that her little patient would make a good recovery and voicing the opinion that travel broadened the mind and would Rose be sure and keep her money in a safe place. 'And let me know how you get on, my dear,' she finished. 'We shall both be glad to hear from you; here's Maggie.'

Maggie disliked the telephone; her voice, faintly apprehensive, came over the wire hesitantly. 'Take care now,' she begged Rose, 'and don't eat too much of that nasty foreign food. Come back soon, love.'

Rose put the receiver back; they were dears, the pair of them, the moment she got back when she had days off she'd go and see them. She pondered the problem of ringing her stepmother and decided against it. There was little point in it, neither she nor her new husband took any interest in her, nor she in them.

It was getting on for three o'clock; she went along to the pantry and made herself a pot of tea and sat drinking it, checking over in her mind that she had everything she might need with her. She tidied the tea things away, went to her room and collected her case and shoulder bag and crossed the street to the hospital. She was early but the Rolls was there in the forecourt with Mr Werdmer ter Sane at the wheel. As soon as he saw her he came to meet her, took her case and put it in the boot and ushered her into the front seat.

'I don't intend to stop on the way,' he informed her, his tone so friendly that she found herself agreeing at once. 'We can get a sandwich and coffee on the hovercraft. You've had lunch?'

'Yes, thank you.' The shepherd's pie and milk pudding still felt solid inside her. She settled herself without fuss and sat back in the comfortable seat; she had little intention of talking and remembering his remarks to Miss Timms, she imagined that he probably felt the same. And indeed, he had nothing to say until they were clear of the last suburbs and racing towards Dover.

'This case,' he began, 'I'll fill in a few details. The little chap's name is Duert, he's two and four months, a healthy specimen and being sensibly brought up. He's lively and big for his age ... his father's a big man. He has a posterior fossa fracture and there is a good deal of swelling of the brain. I have operated to relieve this but there was a CSF leak and I'm worried that there might be a latent infection. He is in the children's hospital in Amsterdam; his parents live in The Hague, but I can keep a closer eye on him if he's on my ward. He's in a side ward and you will be doing day duty, probably your free time will be curtailed for a few days; it will be made up to you later. His father is the director of a hospital in The Hague but he visits whenever he can spare a minute. His mother expects their second child within a few weeks; she's a level-headed girl and realises that there is little that she can do at the moment. That is why she begged for an English nurse; she feels that she can phone you and talk about Duert. She visits him each evening with her husband and she is convinced that he will recover . . .'

'And you? What do you think?' asked Rose.

'He has a very good chance but it depends largely on good nursing now. You have nursed similar cases?'

'Oh, yes. Won't there be a language difficulty?'

'No. At least not in the hospital, the night nurse is English-speaking and so is the ward sister. I doubt if you could hold a general conversation with them, but you will find that they understand medical terms. My registrar speaks excellent English. You will have a room in the nurses' hostel and when Duert goes home I hope that you will be able to go with him until such time as Christina has got things organised.'

'Christina?'

'His mother. They have a splendid nanny, not a trained nurse though, but able to take over from you once Duert is out of danger.'

After that he was silent, leaving her to her own thoughts. She couldn't help but reflect that if it had been Sadie sitting beside him, he might have found something to talk about. He was treating her pleasantly enough but with, she suspected, indifference. To be expected, she told herself philosophically, after all, she was a nurse, being driven to a case by the patient's doctor; and the patient was all that they had in common.

She hadn't been on a hovercraft before; she found it exhilarating. She ate the sandwiches and drank the coffee offered her and sat composedly while Mr Werdmer ter Sane studied the papers he drew from his brief case.

It was still light when they landed, and since the land was flat and the sky wide, she was able to see around her. She longed to ask what this was and that was, but her companion, beyond making sure that she was comfortable, had little to say. Only as they slowed to go through the lighted outskirts of Amsterdam, did he observe, 'A very restful travelling companion—no girlish exclamations of delight, no endless questions about windmills and clogs, no demands to know when we should arrive. I must congratulate you, Nurse Comely.'

To which she made no reply at all.

Once through the suburbs, the city took on the

enchantment she had remembered from her brief visit. The sky was clear and starlit, silhouetting the gabled houses against the deep blue above, and once they were away from the main streets, there were only the street lamps reflected in the canal water.

She hadn't asked where they were going; she hoped just for a moment that they would go to his house first, but she was to be disappointed. They left the quiet old streets presently and turned back into the main part of the city. A short cut, she guessed, and knew that she was right when they turned into a wide courtyard with the hospital, quite unmistakable, beyond. Mr Werdmer ter Sane switched off the engine. 'Well, here we are,' he observed quietly, and got out to open her door and usher her through the wide entrance.

There was no waiting about; he lifted a hand to the porter on duty and led the way to a row of lifts. They got out on the second floor and Rose followed silently as he trod unhurriedly a long wide corridor and through swing doors.

It was very quiet; there were wards on either side, their doors open and night lights burning and the shadowy figures of nurses going to and fro. Mr Werdmer ter Sane tapped on a door at the end of the corridor and went in.

There was a cot in the room, barely visible in the dim light, surrounded by all the impedimenta of post-operative equipment. Sitting side by side in chairs drawn up to the cot were two people. They turned their heads as Rose and Mr Werdmer ter Sane went in and the man got up. He was a big man, heavily built and tall, and he looked tired and very anxious.

'Sybren—you've made good time.' He looked at Rose and smiled. He was good-looking and his eyes

were very blue. 'And this will be our English nurse.'
He put out his hand and then he put a hand on his
wife's shoulder. 'Chrissy, now you will be able to
sleep.'

The girl took her eyes from the small figure in the
cot. Mrs ter Brandt wasn't pretty, but her eyes were a
lovely grey in a white face. She smiled at Rose.

'Thank you for coming.' She got up and offered a
hand. 'You're from St Bride's, aren't you? The best
nurse they have got, Sybren says. Little Duert will be
all right now.'

Rose said comfortingly, 'I'm sure he will and I
promise you I'll look after him, Mevrouw ter Brandt.'

The two men had turned aside to talk but presently
Doctor ter Brandt said, 'We're going home now,
darling—Sybren will take a look at Duert and explain
things to . . .' He glanced over to Rose. 'May I call you
Rose? She will come on duty in the morning and you
can phone her then and come and see Duert later in
the day. And I promise you we won't pull any wool
over your eyes, darling.'

Rose saw the look which passed between them;
loving and trusting and very understanding. It must
be awful, she thought, as she wished them a calm good
night.

Mr Werdmer ter Sane closed the door. 'Now, before
we find Night Sister and get you settled, let us go over
the notes . . .' He gave her a sharp glance. 'You are not
too tired? There will be a meal for you presently, but
this is too good an opportunity to miss.'

He went and looked at the unconscious child,
examining him gently. 'He's no worse, but he's by no
means out of the wood. I want every smallest change
noted and I want to be told at once. I'll give you a
phone number and you are to ring me without waiting

to report to the ward sister. Tell her, of course, but I want to know first. You understand?'

Rose nodded. She was tired and hungry but since Mr Werdmer ter Sane didn't appear to be either, she supposed she would have to forget that for the time being. He began to go over the case papers with her in great detail, and when he had finished, 'You understand all that, Nurse? Have you any questions?'

'No, not at present,' she told him and he turned to ring the bell by the cot. 'Night Nurse,' he told her, 'while Duert and Christina are here she isn't needed.'

The girl who came in quietly was big and fair-haired and pretty. She said something to Mr Werdmer ter Sane and smiled at Rose, who said 'Hullo', and offered a hand.

'Wiebeke—Rose,' he said briefly. He went on in Dutch so that Rose couldn't understand but when he had finished he said, 'I was telling Wiebeke that you will be on duty at seven o'clock in the morning. She speaks English but if you have any hang-ups for heaven's sake give me a ring.' He turned back to the night nurse, saying over his shoulder, 'Wait a minute, will you? I'll introduce you to Night Sister.'

It was five minutes before he had talked to Wiebeke and taken another look at the child. Rose said good night to the other girl and followed him back the way they had come and into a small office. Night Sister was a large bony woman with a calm, middle-aged face. She got up from the desk as they went in, smiled at them both and asked in English, 'This is our English nurse?' She shook hands and listened while Mr Werdmer ter Sane talked and then said, 'We will go at once to the hostel, you must be tired, and tomorrow morning at seven o'clock we will see you here on duty. We are glad to welcome you, Nurse Comely.'

She glanced towards their companion. 'You are going home, Doctor?'

'No, not just yet. I'll wish you good night.' He nodded to them both and walked back the way they had come.

'He is anxious,' explained Night Sister, 'he is—how do you say?—godfather to the little Duert. We go this way.'

Rose hardly noticed where they were going; she was famished and wanted a bed and a bath more than anything else in the world. It was several floors down and any number of passages before they went through a door and up more stairs leading to silent corridors lined with doors. Night Sister opened one. 'Your room, Zuster Comely.'

Rose went past her into a small, nicely furnished room, very clean and bright. 'I'm not a sister,' she said shyly. 'Only a staff nurse.'

Night Sister laughed. 'Ah, but here we call all nurses "Zuster" and the sister is "Hoofdzuster". The bathroom is at the end of this passage, there are six— but first someone will be coming very soon with your supper. And in the morning a nurse will show you where to go. You will be called at six o'clock.' She smiled again. 'I hope you will be happy with us. Good night.'

Left to herself, Rose unpacked and then since her supper hadn't arrived, undressed and got into her dressing-gown. She was brushing her hair when there was a tap on the door and a young woman came in with a tray. She nodded and smiled and put the tray on the writing-desk under the window and when Rose asked, 'What shall I do with the tray?' giggled gently, shrugged her shoulders and went away.

The supper was all that she could have wished for:

soup and savoury pancakes and a bowl of yoghurt and a jug of piping-hot coffee. Rose disposed of everything and crept down to the bathroom past the silent rooms. The water was hot and she lay for a while going over the events of the day, then mindful of the early start in the morning she got out reluctantly and presently was back in her room. A rather nice room, she thought drowsily, putting out the bedside light.

It seemed that she had only just shut her eyes when she was being gently shaken awake. A girl was bending over her and she sat up in bed, not sure where she was for the moment. The girl smiled. 'You get up,' she said, and 'I fetch you.' At the door she paused, clutching her dressing-gown about her. 'Okay?'

'Okay,' said Rose and jumped out of bed.

She was fetched by a whole bunch of girls who shook hands in a friendly fashion and exclaimed over the old fashioned uniform St Bride's nurses still wore. They bore her along with them, back down the stairs and into the hospital and then underground. The canteen was large and cheerful with tables for four or six and a long counter along one end. Rose, who was hungry again, was disappointed to see that there was only bread and butter and slices of cheese and great urns of coffee. Perhaps just as well, she decided, catching sight of the clock, there wouldn't be time for any more.

Conversation was sparse but friendly at the table, because eating and drinking were more important than gossip and presently they swept her along once more and left her at the children's unit.

Rose went in through the swing doors to the familiar sounds of shouts and cries and the general din made by a number of toddlers even if they weren't so well. The office she had been taken to was close by, she tapped on the door and went in.

Night Sister was there, still on duty, and there was another, younger woman with her who got up from the stool she was sitting on.

'Nurse Comely. I am glad to meet you. I am the hoofdzuster of the ward and presently I will explain your duty times to you, but now I think it best if you go to relieve the night nurse, please. Mr Werdmer ter Sane will be in presently and he will wish to see you also.'

Rose went along the corridor and opened the end-room door. Wiebeke was sitting at a small table filling in the charts, but she looked round as Rose went in and beamed at her. 'You have slept? Yes? We have had a good night. Duert is still unconscious. I tell you the report now?'

Wiebeke's English was sometimes quaint, but understandable, besides the treatments and feeds and charts were the same as she was used to at St Bride's, only in another language. When she had made quite sure that she had understood Wiebeke's report, Rose bade her goodbye and set about her day's tasks.

She had just finished giving Duert a nasal feed when Mr Werdmer ter Sane came in. His good morning was quiet and he went at once to look and having seen the child sat down to read through the reports and charts.

When he had finished he asked: 'Have you anything to report, Nurse Comely?'

'Nothing more than is written there, sir.'

He got up and went over to the cot. 'Let's see now ...' He went over the small body very carefully, looking for some sign of awakening consciousness, and found none. Presently he straightened up. 'I'll be back presently,' he told her. 'Mevrouw ter Brandt will be coming in this afternoon. I'd be obliged if you will be here when she comes; it will make things easier for her if she can talk to you.'

There wasn't a great deal to do but she needed to keep the little boy under constant surveillance. She was relieved briefly for her midday meal and soon after she returned Christina ter Brandt arrived. Her husband and Mr Werdmer ter Sane came with her. They went to bend over the cot until Dr ter Brandt said quietly: 'Sit down, darling, he's doing as well as we hoped. Sybren and I are going to have a talk in Sister's office. Shall I get someone to send in a pot of tea? You two girls can have a chat while we are gone.'

He laid a large comforting hand on his wife's shoulder and smiled at Rose.

Left to themselves, Rose brought her stool close to the cot so that she could watch little Duert. 'He's a lovely boy,' she said in her pleasant voice. 'Has he blue eyes?'

'Like his father's.' Christina patted herself. 'This one's to be a girl with grey eyes like mine. I don't mind what colour they are but Duert has set his heart on it.' She looked away for a moment. 'You haven't seen any sign at all?'

'Not yet,' said Rose gently, 'it's always a long business, isn't it? We've had several like Duert at St Bride's; they took their time but they all went home fit and well.'

Christina ter Brandt smiled rather shakily. 'Bless you, what a comfort you are. You think he'll—he'll be none the worse?'

'Yes, I think that. I think Mr Werdmer ter Sane thinks that too.'

'He's a tower of strength. You met him when you were on holiday?'

'Well, yes. I banged on his door because we were lost and there was a fearful storm and he very kindly gave us tea.'

'Who's us?'

She wasn't sure if her companion was listening, her eyes were on her small son, but Rose went on talking comfortably, anything was better than sitting in silence. 'Sadie—one of my friends. She is a dear and very, very pretty—she is marvellous with children too. She and Mr Werdmer ter Sane got on awfully well . . .'

'And you don't?'

'Oh, yes, of course.' Rose remembered his opinion of her and went a delicate pink and Christina gave her a second look. 'He's not very easy to know,' she said casually, 'plenty of girl friends when he has the time for them, but no sign of getting married. Did he fall for your friend Sadie?'

'Well, I think he might have done if they had seen more of each other.'

'I am glad it's you . . . may I call you Rose? I think you are the sort of person who won't get impatient if I burst into tears or have sudden hysterics.'

'Indeed I won't.' Rose got up and eased the small body gently from one side to the other, took the pulse in the flaccid wrist, charted it and sat down again. A tray of tea was brought in then and Rose was asked to pour out.

'This is fun,' said Christina ter Brandt, taking her cup. 'We've heaps of friends but I haven't wanted to see any of them since—since . . .' She took a sip of tea. 'But it's great to be able to sit here with Duert and have someone to talk to who understands what's happened to him.'

In a little while Dr ter Brandt came back, took

another look at his little son, passed a gentle time of day with Rose and took his wife away.

They met Sybren in the corridor. 'She's a darling,' said Christina to him. 'Do you know I feel quite different now she is here. She's so sure he's going to get better and so—so sensible and kind. When Duert is well enough to come home, she must come too, just for a bit,' and at his look of doubt, 'don't say it can't be done because between the pair of you, you can do anything you've set your heart on.' She looked at her husband. 'Duert, dear, please . . .'

He had an arm round her shoulders. 'Provided Rose will agree, we'll get her by hook or by crook.' He looked at his friend. 'Well, what do you say, Sybren?'

'She is a good nurse and if you want her, we'll arrange things.'

Christina said thoughtfully, 'Would you rather have had her friend—what was her name—Sadie? Very pretty, Rose tells me. And a good nurse too.'

He smiled down at her. 'Very pretty, but I don't think we could better our Rose; unflappable and sensible and somehow slides into place without any fuss.' He bent to kiss her cheek. 'We'll have good news for you, Chrissy, just be patient.'

Rose was patient too; perhaps the small child's life depended on her regular frequent observations, the careful taking of pulse, checking the slow breathing, the level of consciousness. She was relieved for her meals but that was all, but she had known that already; when she went off duty in the evening she had her supper and then went for a brisk walk, sometimes by herself, more often with one or other of the nurses. They were friendly girls but she had little time to get to know them. Wiebeke she saw morning and evening, but beyond giving each other the report they wasted no time. Little Duert's life depended on constant observation until he regained consciousness and they both knew it. For the next few days nothing else mattered.

Christina ter Brandt came each day to sit by her little son's cot and hold his hand while she talked to Rose. That she was happily married was evident, just as it was evident that she was whole-heartedly loved. Rose, after a few days, found herself liking her very much, just as she liked Dr ter Brandt. Two people such as they were deserved a miracle.

Mr Werdmer ter Sane came twice a day to study the charts carefully and examine his small patient. He had little to say to Rose although he was always pleasant and careful to enquire as to her welfare, enquiries she brushed aside just as pleasantly. She was beginning to feel the lack of exercise and change of scene but she had no intention of saying so.

It was on the fourth day, half way through the morning, that she noticed the faintest of movements and the little boy's breathing changed slightly from slow and shallow to a steadier rhythm. She went to the phone in a flash and asked for Mr Werdmer ter Sane to come at once, and then whisked back to the cotside, taking another look before ringing Sister's office. Only there was no one there to answer. Rose went back to the cot, took down the side and perched close to the small form. It seemed to her that the level of unconsciousness was lighter even in those few minutes. She stroked the little hand she was holding and began to sing very softly: nursery rhymes, one after the other, and was rewarded by the flicker of an eyelid. When the door opened and Mr Werdmer ter Sane came quietly in, she flapped a hand at him and went on singing 'Hey diddle diddle, the cat and the fiddle'. She had a small high voice a little breathless now with excitement. 'The cow jumped over the moon,' she went on, aware that he was standing behind her.

The cherub in the cot opened two astonishingly blue eyes, said sleepily 'lickle dog', and closed them again.

'Oh, my goodness me,' said Rose in a whisper. She took the large hand on the counterpane beside her and gave it a squeeze, quite unaware of what she was doing. But only for a moment; she dropped it like a hot brick and stood up, to recite very accurately exactly what had occurred.

Mr Werdmer ter Sane grunted and bent over the little boy who stirred under his gentle touch and then opened his eyes again. He said something in Dutch and straightened to his great height again. 'I do believe we're coming out of the wood, Rose.'

Very much to her surprise he bent and kissed her cheek. 'Good girl.' He went to the phone and made several calls and very soon Sister was there as well as his registrar. The three of them talked quietly and then the two men examined the child very gently. Rose stood a little apart. Sister was there, handling things and dealing with their needs and there was nothing for her to do. Sister and the registrar went presently and Mr Werdmer ter Sane asked her to stay by the cot while he phoned and then presently he gave her careful instructions and went away too.

There was little enough to do; only watch carefully and carry out the usual nursing chores. It was half an hour later that he came back and this time he had the ter Brandts with him.

Rose didn't say anything; indeed they weren't aware of anyone else except the little boy in the cot. She slid away to the desk at the window and turned her back and was surprised when Mr Werdmer ter Sane joined her.

There wasn't anything much to see; a variety of gabled roofs and an enormous number of chimney pots and above them, a wide pale blue sky. She stared out at them and wished she could think of something to say and presently he went away again without having uttered a word, back to the cot at the other side of the room and now it was Christina beside her.

'Rose, oh Rose, you don't know how happy I am. Oh, my dear, we're so grateful and thankful.' She turned a tear-stained face to her. 'We'll never be able to thank you enough.'

'But I haven't done anything,' said Rose, feeling awkward.

'Oh, yes, you have. You'd made up your mind that little Duert was going to get better and you've had no off-duty and you've had your eyes on him all the time. That was clever, singing the nursery rhymes. Sybren says he's not out of the wood yet but it's time and careful nursing. You'll stay, won't you? I can't nurse him myself, but I know he is safe with you.'

'Of course, I'll stay. I am so happy for you and your husband, you must be in the seventh heaven. And I'll take great care of him, I promise you, and Wiebeke is wonderful, you know. You'll be able to sleep at night now.'

'Yes, oh yes.' Christina looked up at her husband who had just joined her. He smiled a little at her and then looked at Rose. 'We are in your debt for the rest of our lives, Rose.'

When they had gone she took up her station by the cot again. Perhaps there would be days ahead when not much progress would be made, but it was a start.

She took Duert's hand in hers once more and started to sing 'Ride a cock horse' in her soft little voice.

Mr Werdmer ter Sane, coming back up the corridor, paused to listen outside the door. He frowned heavily, aware of annoyance because Rose, that most uninteresting of girls, disturbed him. A pity that Christina had set her heart on having her back home when little Duert was well enough to leave hospital. Hopefully, she wouldn't need to stay long.

CHAPTER THREE

THERE was a steady improvement in little Duert; he slept for the greater part of the day, but the intervals of wakefulness lengthened and by the end of a week he could be lifted carefully on to his mother's lap when she came to see him. No permanent brain damage, Mr Werdmer ter Sane assured her, little Duert was going to be perfectly all right. Even now, he pointed out gently, he was smiling at his mother and father and talking a little. Time and patience, he counselled Christina. Rose wasn't sure if he was quite so hopeful with Doctor ter Brandt although there was nothing in the men's manner to betray their thoughts; she knew it was important to keep Christina happy and at the same time no attempt was made to pull the wool over her eyes; the little boy was indeed making progress but he still had a long way to go and she didn't relax her watchfulness one particle.

It was at the end of a sunny afternoon, when the ter Brandts had gone home, that Mr Werdmer ter Sane came back to talk to her. Rather to her surprise he wanted to have her opinion of little Duert's progress.

She didn't hurry to answer; he wanted facts, not guesses and too-hopeful opinions. 'He's going ahead, but very slowly. Well, I know progress is slow in these cases but I dare say it seems slower because we're all so anxious to see him well again. However, he's beginning to enjoy his food, he listens when I talk and sing to him and he loves his parents' visits.' Rose paused and looked up at the grave face. 'What are you afraid of, Sir?'

'Ah, discerning Rose, meningitis, so keep your intelligent eye open, will you, for the next week. After that we should be all right. No sign of vomiting? No twitching?'

'Fits?' said Rose. 'No, none at all. After fourteen days he should be safe, shouldn't he?'

'Yes, three, no, four days to go. Are you getting tired? You are not getting your proper off-duty, but you do realise that Christina trusts you completely.' He smiled suddenly. 'So do I, Rose. Bear with us for a few more days, then you shall have time to yourself.'

The smile had shaken her; she had glimpsed a man she hadn't known, quite different from the austere politeness she had come to expect.

'I'm quite all right,' she assured him. 'I go for a walk every evening and I wouldn't know what to do with myself even if I were free.'

'It's nice of you to say so, but I find that hard to believe; you knew how to make the most of your stay here when we first met.'

'Yes—well, Sadie was with me, she wanted to see everything too.'

He cast a quick look at the sleeping child in his cot. 'Ah, yes, Sadie. And how is she? A very pretty girl, I was sorry I had no time to see more of her when I came over to St Bride's.'

'She was sorry too.' So he had fallen for Sadie after all, perhaps not all that deeply, but it would have been nice for them both if they could have got to know each other better. 'It was such a pity,' went on Rose rather recklessly, 'that Miss Timms insisted on me; Sadie would have loved to come and I'm sure you would have liked to have had her here . . .'

'You preposterous girl,' he exploded with a force whose very quietness was blistering. 'What an extraordinary thing to say to me. And how, now I come to think about it, did you know that Miss Timms urged you upon me?'

Rose kept her eyes on his face, quite petrified inside although she looked her usual calm self. 'I heard her. The office door was open as I reached it and she has a very ringing kind of voice. I heard you too.' She tried a conciliatory smile and met a bleak stare. 'I didn't mean to listen. I'm sorry you had to have me when you wanted Sadie.'

He said in an even voice: 'You were brought here to nurse little Duert: something which you are doing admirably. You can have little leisure to, er—take an interest in my own wishes, Nurse Comely. I suggest that we confine ourselves and our conversation to the needs and treatment of the patient.'

Rose went a very bright pink but she met his bland look; it wasn't only bland, there was amused mockery there too, which made it much worse. She sought worriedly for something to say and drew a blank; Providence came to her aid in the shape of his bleep which sent him to the telephone and then, with no more than a nod, out of the room.

Left with her patient, Rose bustled quietly about her duties. Duert was sleeping and there wasn't a great deal to do for another hour other than the regular observations. She sat down by the cot where she could watch him and went over her conversation with Mr Werdmer ter Sane. A most unsatisfactory one, she thought sadly. Her stepmother had never made any bones about her inability to interest even the most ordinary of young men; she could see how right that lady had been, for not only did Mr Werdmer ter Sane

have no interest in her whatsover, he appeared to
dislike her as well. She reminded herself that she
didn't like him either but the thought didn't give her
the uplift in spirits she expected; it left her gloomier
than ever.

But she was a sensible girl; moaning would get her
nowhere, and little Duert was showing signs of waking.
She went and sat on the side of his cot and began on
the string of nursery rhymes he enjoyed and was
rewarded presently by his chuckles.

Mr Werdmer ter Sane brought his registrar with
him that evening and it was after the pair of them had
examined the little boy and checked the charts that the
registrar paused beside Rose to enquire if she was
going anywhere that evening?

'Me, no,' said Rose surprised.

'Then perhaps you will come to my home and have
supper with my wife and me? My wife would like to
meet you.'

Rose pinkened with pleasure. 'Oh, would she? How
nice. I'd love to come.'

'You go off duty at seven o'clock? I will be outside
the hospital at eight o'clock. We have a flat not far
away.'

'That's awfully kind of you. I'll be ready.' Her eyes
sparkled with excitement; the other nurses had been
friendly and gone with her for walks in the evening or
made rather laborious conversation round the TV but
this was something different. She beamed at him and
then stopped smiling as she caught Mr Werdmer ter
Sane's eye. The mockery was there again. Well, let
him mock. Her 'good night, sir', was uttered with a
light-heartedness which sent his eyebrows up.

It was well past seven o'clock by the time she had
given Wiebeke the report and detailed little Duert's

progress; by now she had learnt her way around the hospital and skipped along its corridors and down its stairs intent on getting to her room. She had reached the bottom of the last staircase before she saw Mr Werdmer ter Sane watching her from a few feet away.

'You are late, Nurse Comely?'

'There is the report to give,' she pointed out, 'and Wiebeke and I spend a minute or two talking to Duert so that he knows I'm going and she is coming.' She didn't wait for his answer but skipped past him, along the passage to the nurses' home and through the door. He stood where she had left him and a look of faint surprise was on his face and presently a reluctant smile tugged at his strong mouth.

Some hours later, lying in her bed, comfortably sleepy, Rose reviewed her evening. It had been a delightful one. Wim Becke had been waiting for her and had driven her in his old Citroen to a quiet little backwater of narrow streets where he had a flat. The house was tall and thin and, like most of the old houses, extended back from the street to a depth of several rooms. He lived on the second floor and they mounted narrow twisting stairs to reach it. The landing was small but once inside the tiny hall opened out into a long narrow passage with all the rooms on one side. Wim's wife had welcomed her warmly in an English not to be compared with his own rather pedantic speech, and they had all spent some time admiring the small girl, already asleep, before sitting down in the pleasant, low-ceilinged living-room to have their supper. And after the meal they had sat and talked and plied Rose with advocaat, and Marijke had suggested that when Rose was free again, she might like to spend a few hours with her. 'We can go to the shops,' she offered, 'they are not too far away and perhaps you wish to buy.'

Rose hadn't left too late, Wim worked a long day now and was on call for a good deal of the time. 'But of course, Mr Werdmer ter Sane is also always available unless he is out of the country. He is splendid with children as you have seen.'

'He is also Wilma's godfather,' interpolated Marijke proudly. Rose had murmured suitably. Obviously he was thought of very highly in Wim's small household.

The next few days went uneventfully by; little Duert, now that he was fully conscious, was going ahead by leaps and bounds. Mr Werdmer ter Sane came and went, often accompanied by Doctor ter Brandt and Christina, but whether he was accompanied or alone, he had little to say to Rose. On one evening, out for her usual brisk walk before bedtime, she had seen him driving his Rolls. There had been a girl sitting beside him, a sparkling dark creature, laughing and gesticulating. That much Rose had seen as they went past. Mr Werdmer ter Sane had been looking ahead, faintly smiling, and of course he hadn't seen her standing on the pavement.

Only of course he had.

The crucial two weeks were up the following morning; he examined the little boy even more thoroughly than usual before turning to Wim.

'I do believe that there will be no after effects; he should go ahead fast now, but we must take care for another few weeks. I'll talk to Duert about getting him home—the sooner the better now, you agree?'

He glanced across the cot to where Rose was standing. 'You have done a good job of work, Rose. I must remember to tell Miss Timms when next I see her, perhaps it will compensate her a little for the inconvenience of borrowing you.'

He and Wim spoke Dutch after that and she set about settling little Duert for his nap and presently they wandered away with brief nods. At the door Sister appeared to ask for Wim's advice about something and led him away and instead of following them Mr Werdmer ter Sane turned back into the room.

'Do you always go walking alone in the evenings?' he wanted to know.

Rose fastened the cot sides and gave him a brief glance. 'Yes.' And then, 'Not quite always; if there is someone off duty who isn't going out they go with me.'

'You are not lonely?'

She had been lonely for some years: she had plenty of friends, everyone liked her but no one loved her. Of course she was lonely. 'Not in the least,' she assured him.

She was glad to see him go.

Christina and Duert ter Brandt came the next morning. 'Sybren's busy,' explained Duert smoothly. 'He told me last night that we could have little Duert home next week.'

'That is marvellous news,' said Rose. She sat Christina down in a chair by the cot where the little boy was having his morning nap. 'He's made such strides.' She glanced at Christina who looked happy but tired. 'You have a nanny, don't you? Isn't the baby due next week?' she added hastily, fearful of sounding as though she was prying. 'Won't he be pleased to have a baby sister . . .?'

Duert ter Brandt agreed pleasantly. 'Only there is a snag. Christina would like you to come back with us, just for a couple of weeks while she is getting back on her feet. Nanny's a treasure, but she's not a trained nurse.'

Rose said at once: 'Oh, I should have loved that—to see little Duert really fit again, but I'm supposed to go back to St Bride's—Sister Cummins was quite annoyed at me coming here, you know.'

'Ah yes! the militant gorgon on children's surgical—I've met her. Rose, if I could manage to persuade her and your principal nursing officer to let you stay another couple of weeks, would you come back with little Duert? I know you've had no off-duty, but once he's settled in, you shall have your free time made up to you threefold.' He took a look at his wife. 'Chrissy, it's your turn, darling.'

'Please come, Rose,' Christina begged. 'If you are there looking after him, I can have the baby in peace of mind. Please say you'll come?' She paused. 'Then if anything should go wrong you'll be there to look after him.'

'Nothing's going to go wrong,' declared Rose, 'and if Miss Timms will let me, I'll come.'

Little Duert woke up then and was sat carefully on his father's knee. 'We are eternally grateful,' said Duert ter Brandt. 'I'll set about seeing everyone concerned.'

Hoofdzuster came in then, followed by a ward maid with a tray of coffee, and Doctor ter Brandt suggested with a gentle authority which no one would have dreamt of querying that he and Sister might have a little chat while Rose and Christina sat apart. 'There must be an awful lot you want to know,' he concluded kindly to Rose.

He was a dear, mused Rose, going to sit by Christina, and she, who had taught herself not to be envious because it was such a waste of time, was envious of Christina. To be loved like that; for no reason at all Mr Werdmer ter Sane's face rose before her eyes and she shied away from it. 'What will Mr Werdmer ter Sane say?' she asked before she could stop herself.

'He'll agree,' said Christina instantly. He had agreed on the previous evening when he had gone to The Hague to dine with them, indeed, more than that, he had suggested it in the first place. 'He thinks very highly of you as a nurse, Rose. And so do we. I'm so glad you'll come. Now I'll tell you something of where we live.'

Which took some time; Hoofdzuster went away presently and then the ter Brandts, and Rose was on her own again with the sleeping child. Little Duert woke presently and they embarked together on the childish games which delighted him.

The week slid away, the weather got warmer, little Duert became increasingly active and Mr Werdmer ter Sane paid him frequent visits, coolly polite to Rose, merely enquiring if she was content with the details she had been given by Christina and bearing a message from Dr ter Brandt that he had arranged everything satisfactorily. It only remained for her to write to Aunt Millicent explaining the situation and assuring her that she was perfectly content to remain for as long as was required.

Aunt Millicent wrote back by return; a sensible, no-nonsense letter pointing out that Rose should take full advantage of her stay in Holland and whenever possible see all that there was to see. Moreover, she should be thankful that she had been trained in a profession which was doing some good in the world. This rather tart missive ended with the hope that Rose would pay a visit as soon as possible when she returned to England for both she and Maggie were missing her. It made no mention of the letter which Aunt Millicent had received from Mr Werdmer ter Sane, explaining Rose's extended stay in his country, and pointing out that it was largely due to her devoted care that his small patient had recovered. Aunt Millicent had read the letter several times and become quite thoughtful over it.

When the time came Rose was quite sorry to leave the hospital; she had made some friends there in her limited free time, she had liked the Hoofdzuster and she got on well with Wim. She had even begun to have a limited knowledge of Amsterdam, exploring rather gingerly on her short evening walks. Now she would have to begin all over again in The Hague, but that might be fun for Christina had told her that it was a charming place with a great deal to see, near the sea and with some splendid shops. 'And heaven knows you haven't had a chance to buy so much as a newspaper,' she had declared. 'I promise you that just as soon as we are organised at home you shall have your lost free time made up to you.'

Dr ter Brandt came to fetch them, explaining in his quiet way that Christina had chosen that very day to start the baby. 'It won't be just yet,' he added, 'and nothing would do but that I should collect you as we had arranged. I would have asked Sybren to bring you but he's in Brussels for a couple of days.'

So Rose wasted no time in getting her patient into the car with all his bits and pieces, together with her case, and then she got in beside him. 'How long does it take to get to The Hague?' she asked anxiously.

'It's forty miles more or less. About thirty minutes on the motorway.'

They did it in twenty-nine and Rose guessed that under Dr ter Brandt's calm he was on edge to get home just as fast as he could. All the same, when they arrived at the substantial mansion on the outskirts of The Hague he took time to introduce the short stout man as Corvinus his butler and told her that he would assist her in any way he could, before he asked a quick question in his own language. Apparently the answer was satisfactory for the doctor carried his small son indoors and upstairs, bidding Rose follow. The staircase was wide and led to a gallery above, lined with doors and with several passages leading from it. A door was flung open as they reached the head of the stairs and a small plump figure bounced out.

'Nanny,' said Dr ter Brandt. 'Forgive me, Rose, but I must go to my wife.'

This left her smiling uncertainly at Nanny with little Duert, crowing with delight in her arms.

Nanny smiled back. She said something in Dutch and held out a hand and Rose proffered her own, rather awkwardly because of little Duert. Then she handed the little boy over to the other woman and was rewarded by her sudden smile. 'I'll fetch the things in,' said Rose, and trotted off downstairs again to find Corvinus making his way across the hall, burdened by all the impedimenta they had brought from the hospital.

He gravely refused help. 'And if you will come with me,' he begged her, to her great relief speaking a quite tolerable English, 'I will show you the nursery and your room. I understand that Nanny will be looking after the baby. Little Duert is in the night nursery and your room is next to it.'

'The baby?' asked Rose quickly.

'Very shortly, nurse. So my wife tells me. She is the

housekeeper here. She is English and her name is Sally and I'm sure she will be glad to help you in any way.'

Rose beamed at him, feeling at home. 'Nanny doesn't speak English?'

'No, nurse. She is from Friesland. But she is a most friendly person and very glad that you will be here to look after little Duert while she helps Mevrouw with the baby.'

She followed him across the hall and up the staircase then across the wide landing and into a passage leading from it. There were three doors, and he opened the middle one. 'Your room, Nurse. As soon as Sally is free she will come to welcome you. We are at the moment rather—rather . . .'

'At sixes and sevens?' asked Rose helpfully and was rewarded by his ready smile. 'Don't bother about me, I'll unpack and then go and see Nanny.'

Unpacking didn't take long; she tidied her person, explored her charming room and the splendid bathroom leading from it, took a look at the nursery and went through the passage to the landing once more. Nanny had come out of a door on the other side of it; Rose tapped and hearing a voice answer went inside. Little Duert was sitting in his high chair, playing with the teddy bear which went everywhere with him, and Nanny was getting ready for the baby. They smiled at each other and Rose dropped a kiss on the little boy's cheek, wondering how on earth they were to communicate.

It wasn't difficult after all; Sally came into the room, she was a plump little woman, her round face beaming. 'Just fancy, Nurse, Mevrouw ter Brandt has just had a little girl. Ever so quick and the doctor was just in time.' Her eyes fell on little Duert. 'And here's our dear boy back home. My goodness, what a happy day. Now if you like to tell me how you would like things arranged I'll see to it. Nanny can't speak a word of English, but she's a dear soul; we're all very pleased to have you here, I can tell you, knowing how you've nursed him well again. I dare say the doctor will be along presently to talk to you. I'll send up some coffee and whatever you want for little Duert.' She paused for breath and Rose said, 'You're awfully kind, I do hope I shan't make any extra work.'

'Lor, no, Nurse, there's enough of us and to spare.' She trotted away and Rose went to look at the little boy. He seemed perfectly happy and had settled down just as though he had never been away from home. He would have dinner shortly and then have his nap, just as he had in the hospital; Mr Werdmer ter Sane had made it very clear that he was to be kept quiet, but she saw no difficulty there; he was as placid as his father.

She was piling bricks for him, hoping that Nanny, sitting and knitting at the table, wouldn't be jealous, when Dr ter Brandt came in. He had a bottle under his arm and three glasses in his hand.

'A daughter,' he told them, 'a darling little girl who will be as beautiful as Chrissy. They're both asleep, Rose. I'm so sorry that you should arrive into such a disorganised household. Will you drink the baby's health—and Chrissy's, and forgive us?'

He turned to speak to Nanny who chuckled and shook his hand and embarked on quite a speech. When she had finished Rose said, 'Oh, that's marvellous news. Is your wife all right?'

'Wonderfully so.' He smiled at her and she found herself wishing that some day a man would look like that about her. 'Champagne, Rose . . .'

He picked up little Duert in one great arm. 'You

have a very small sister, if she's anything like your mother, she'll twist us all round her thumb.'

The three of them drank their champagne before Dr ter Brandt said, 'Now as to your days, Rose . . .'

He had it all worked out, telling her first and then explaining to Nanny in Fries. 'Nanny doesn't mind in the least if you share the nursery; she will look after the baby and leave you to deal with little Duert; get him out of doors as much as you can and check his progress. Chrissy will be about in a day or so, and once she is, we both want you to have a day to yourself. We've grossly overworked you and intend to put that right.' And when Rose murmured politely, he said, 'I'm going to take this young man to see his mother and sister; if you'll give him his dinner when we get back while Nanny has hers, she'll keep an eye on his rest while we have lunch.'

Later with little Duert fed and already asleep in his cot with Nanny keeping an eye on him, Rose went downstairs for her lunch, a meal she took with Dr ter Brandt. 'Christina's still sleeping,' he explained, 'when she wakes I'm sure that she will want to see you and show you our daughter.'

He glanced at her briefly. 'I've phoned Sybren—he's delighted. He'll be back in a day or so; he'll be keeping an eye on Duert for another week or so. You're quite happy about the boy?'

Rose said that yes she was, and savoured the chocolate mousse Corvinus had served her.

'And we thought,' went on Dr ter Brandt smoothly, 'that you might like a free day on Saturday. I'll be home, Chrissy will be up and around and Nanny can take over for a while. We owe you so much, Rose—never-ending thanks for all you have done . . . We can never pay our debt.'

Rose blushed. 'I've liked looking after little Duert and I've been quite happy. I'd love to have a day off— I'll go to Amsterdam, there is such a lot I've got to see there.'

'A delightful city,' agreed her host, 'but very changed I'm afraid. The smaller streets away from the centre haven't altered but the Dam Square and Kalverstraat have. Once Christina's back on her feet I'm sure she'll want to show you something of The Hague before you leave us.'

Later that afternoon she went to see Christina, sitting up in bed, a pretty colour in her cheeks. 'Isn't it marvellous?' she demanded. 'A daughter, just what we wanted. Little Duert liked her too. Come and look at her.'

A darling baby, Rose conceded, and thought how super to have a baby in your own home with a midwife to look after you and Nanny and a doting husband to fill your room with flowers. She went away presently to fetch her little charge and sat him on the bed, where he stayed until it was time for his tea.

Rose had her dinner alone. Dr ter Brandt had his with his wife so that Rose, once she had settled little Duert for the night, went down to the dining-room where she sat in solitary state at a vast table while Corvinus looked after her. His manner towards her was fatherly so that she was emboldened to talk to him which stopped her feeling lonely.

She settled quickly enough into the routine Dr ter Brandt had mapped out; a very easy routine as it turned out, with nothing else to do but care for little Duert, keep an eye on his progress and play with him in the large garden around the house. And in a couple of days, Christina quite often joined them, lying on a chaise longue in the shade of an old mulberry tree in the centre of the vast lawn, the baby in her pram close by and Nanny keeping an eye on all of them. It was very pleasant; the idea of going back to St Bride's was by no means welcome but had to be faced. Another week, Rose decided, and little Duert would be fully recovered and there would be no more need for him to have her there.

Dr ter Brandt was away for most of the day, although he came home to lunch. There had been no sign of Mr Werdmer ter Sane. Rose kept faithfully to his instructions, made a careful report to Dr ter Brandt each evening and wondered if she would ever see Mr Werdmer ter Sane again.

He came unaccompanied and soft-footed into the nursery, on Friday evening. Rose was presiding over her small charge's supper and had her back to the door. It was little Duert's crow of delight which made her turn round.

She spooned in the next mouthful; her good evening was pleasant and a bit cool which was a waste of time for he came to stand beside her chair and laid a large hand on her shoulder. He said chattily, 'How splendid to come back to such a contented household: Christina with her new baby, Duert like a lord of the earth, Nanny in transports, this little chap almost fit again . . . and you, Rose?'

'I'm very well, thank you,' she said, and shovelled in another spoonful.

'Duert tells me that you are to have a day off on Saturday. What are your plans?'

She said a trifle tartly, 'I shall spend the day in Amsterdam, there are places I want to see . . .' Before he could speak, 'I'm going by train because I want to.'

She wasn't looking at him which was a good thing because he was smiling. 'A splendid notion, you will be glad to get rid of us for a few hours. I suppose you wouldn't consider a companion—Amsterdam is sometimes a little dicey for a solitary stranger.'

'I don't know any companions,' said Rose frostily, 'and I'd like to be by myself.'

'You know me,' observed Mr Werdmer ter Sane surprisingly.

'I'd rather be by myself.' She added belatedly, 'Thank you.'

'You are a stubborn girl, aren't you, Rose? Never mind, but oblige me by not going to the Dam Square and loitering there. It's the gathering place of any number of strange types these days.'

'I'll bear it in mind.' She wiped little Duert's face and got up.

'You have no need to bother about me,' she told him. 'I expect you feel that it's your duty, but I'm quite sensible, you know. Being a plain girl has its advantages.'

He had taken his hand from her shoulder and turned away. Just as though she hadn't spoken he observed, 'I am responsible for you, you will be good enough to do as I ask.'

He went away without waiting for her to answer, which was a good thing because she had made up her mind then and there that the Dam Square would be the high spot of her day. She was a little muddled as to why she had decided that.

He came back later with Dr ter Brandt, and examined the little boy. Rose answered his pleasantly impersonal questions in like tone, agreed quietly that his patient was making splendid progress and listened with disquiet to the doctor telling his friend that of course he would stay to dinner. His invitation was repeated by Christina who had come to join them.

'And don't dare refuse', she begged him, 'this is my
first dinner party since I had the baby, I shall dress up
and so shall Rose.'

Dress up? thought Rose wildly, the only faintly
suitable dress was the linen one, very plain even if a
pretty blue. Second thoughts calmed her though; no
one was likely to notice what she was wearing, the
three of them would have a lot to talk about and
Christina would be the centre of interest.

Once little Duert was in his cot and Nanny had
come back into the room from her supper bearing the
infant and begun on her preparations for the baby's
comfort, Rose got ready for her evening. She had had
her meals with Dr ter Brandt and now that Christina
was about again, with her too, but they had been
informal meals; true, the table had been set with silver
and beautiful glass and the food had been cordon bleu,
but Christina had worn housecoats—luxurious and
glamorous, but nonetheless housecoats, so that Rose
hadn't found her cotton skirts and tops too out of
place. But this evening, she suspected, was to be more
of a social event. She got into the blue linen, dressed
her cloud of hair in the neatest possible fashion, took a
quick look at her charge, and went downstairs, pausing
to carry on one of the peculiar conversations with
Nanny. It was surprising how well they understood
each other and managed never to get into each other's
way. Corvinus was in the hall, hovering to open the
drawing-room door for her with a friendly smile. He
liked Rose, she reminded him of Mevrouw ter Brandt,
quite unlike the midwife, a haughty piece, even if she
was good at her job, ordering him and Sally around
and wanting her meals at all hours. He had been
delighted to see her go. He held the door wide and
thought that Rose looked very nice in her blue dress.

She was the last one down. Christina, in a silk dress which Rose instantly coveted, turned to smile at her as she hesitated just inside the door and the two men got up, the doctor to offer her a chair, making her feel instantly at ease with some gentle remark, while Mr Werdmer ter Sane went over to the drinks table and asked her what she would have.

After that it was all right, they absorbed her into their lighthearted talk until Corvinus appeared to tell them that dinner was served and Christina took Rose's arm and led her across the hall to the dining-room.

They dined superbly; asparagus salad with shrimps, *sole meunière*, roast partridge, followed by meringue tartlets, a glorious concoction of strawberries, meringue and whipped cream, all washed down by the doctor's best champagne, saved for such an occasion. They toasted the baby, little Duert, Christina, and then to her embarrassment, Rose. And afterwards they had coffee in the drawing-room before Rose excused herself on the plea that little Duert would need her attention. 'And I'll be up to say good night to him presently,' said Christina ter Brandt. 'I know he's asleep and I've said good night once all ready ... besides I have to feed the baby ...'

Rose nodded understandingly; even with a faithful Nanny, Christina kept a very motherly eye on her children.

'And then you'll go to bed yourself, darling,' declared her husband. 'Good night, Rose. It has been a pleasant evening.'

Mr Werdmer ter Sane opened the door for her with a casual 'Good night, Rose.' Her 'good night Sir' was uttered with a cold politeness and she heard him draw in his breath sharply. On her way upstairs she wondered if it annoyed him that she hadn't succumbed to his undoubted charm, despite the clear fact that he had no time for her.

She left the house soon after breakfast the next morning having given a careful report to Christina before she went. The doctor would be at home all day and Nanny was there too, she could enjoy herself without worry.

True to her plan, she took a train to Amsterdam, admiring the orderly countryside and the bright clean stations and once at the Central Station she got out and made her way without haste into the busy streets. She had a map with her and she knew where she wanted to go; Damrak first then the Palace, and despite Mr Werdmer ter Sane's warnings, the War Memorial in the Square. There was a large cafe on the corner of Damrak; she had her coffee watching the busy streets and the crowded pavements before crossing the road to the Palace, paying her entrance fee, and touring its grand but chilly interior. Not a place to be cosy in, she decided and went thankfully back into the sunshine. The square was crowded. She stopped to admire the patterned cobbles of its pavement and began to make her way towards the memorial. She didn't hurry; there was a street organ playing near the palace and she paused to look and listen before she sauntered on once more. There was a constant coming and going in the square; people going from Damrak across to Kalverstraat, Rokin or in the opposite direction to Raadhuisstraat. But as she reached its centre she saw that there was a small crowd round the memorial, young people mostly, good naturedly pushing and shoving and shouting to each other. They were sitting on the steps so that it was almost impossible to get through the mass of them. Rose walked round towards the back of the memorial until she thought she saw a gap. There was a man standing on the steps, making a speech though nobody much seemed to be listening and for the first few yards nobody impeded her progress. But then she was brought up short. A small wiry youth, grubby and dressed in jeans and a shirt, blocked her way.

Rose wished him a good morning politely, and asked him to let her pass. 'Just to see the war memorial,' she explained politely, and then, 'do you understand me?'

'Cors I do. What's a pretty girl like you doing 'ere, anyway?'

'I've just told you,' said Rose patiently.

'Nothing ter see.' He glanced round at the youths around them. 'Is there, men?'

They had formed a ring round her. They meant no harm, she told herself, she was in the middle of a public square and she had only to shout . . .

She turned to make her way out of the crowd again but the circle had closed in on her, bent on teasing her.

Mr Werdmer ter Sane, driving slowly up Rokin towards the square, looked casually across to the crowds as he slid the car towards the outer edge of it. The usual lot, he thought idly, and then looked again. He had glimpsed a small figure in a blue dress standing very still.

He wasn't supposed to stop the car there but he did, to cross with quick strides to the fringe of the milling crowd. He clove his way through it, parted the ring of young men with a sweep of his arms and took Rose's arm. He didn't leave immediately, but delivered a short, pithy speech in his own language which his audience answered with sheepish mutterings before they melted sideways to allow him to urge Rose away.

It wasn't until they were crossing the square towards the car that he spoke.

'I am not a man to say "I told you so",' he declared with a snap, 'but you are behaving like a tiresome child, Rose. I told you not to get mixed up with that disreputable lot. Did I not make myself plain?'

'Oh, yes you did—that's why.' She gave him a clear look and added soothingly, 'You have no need to get cross. They wouldn't have bothered me.'

He shook her arm. 'That's where you are wrong. Oh, they wouldn't harm you, I dare say. They would have stolen your purse perhaps, or walked you off to one of the houseboats they live in . . .'

She came to a halt by the car. 'I'm sure you meant well,' she told him kindly. 'Thank you. Now I'm going to the Rijksmuseum.'

His grip didn't slacken. 'Miss Timms must have been out of her mind,' he observed bitterly. 'She said that you were utterly trustworthy and sensible.'

'Well, I hope I am when it comes to being a nurse. But today I'm just me, doing what I want to do.' She took his hand gently from her arm.

'Goodbye, Mr Werdmer ter Sane.'

She walked briskly away, happily unable to hear or understand his softly muttered Dutch swearwords. She would have to go soon, he thought, watching her small straight back disappearing down the street. She was a disturbing influence in his life and he wished whole-heartedly to be rid of it.

CHAPTER FOUR

ON her way back to The Hague that early evening, Rose told herself that she had had a lovely day; she had spent hours looking at the paintings in the Rijksmuseum, had a snack lunch there and then hurried to Rembrandt's house, taken a quick look at the seventeenth-century Munttoren on the way there and then doubled back to go down the Kalverstraat to the Begijnsteeg, leading to the Begijnhof. She stayed there, looking at the fourteenth-century houses encircling the old church, given long ago to the English Reformed community in the city, and then presently wended her way back towards the station. She had seen almost all she had wanted to; the unhidden thought that she would have liked to take another look at Mr Werdmer ter Sane's house was one she didn't choose to contemplate.

Dr ter Brandt had suggested that she should take the particular train she was on and she had to admit that he had judged the time very nicely; she was pleasantly tired and although she had had a cup of tea in one of the many coffee shops, she had had, for the time being at least, quite enough. She would catch a tram from the station and be back at the ter Brandts' house in good time to shower and change her dress.

Corvinus was waiting outside the station and at the sight of him her heart leapt into her throat; something awful must have happened; little Duert—the baby . . . She should never have gone. She almost ran to him.

'Corvinus—is there something wrong? Little Duert . . .?'

'He's grand, Nurse. The doctor asked me to meet this train—he thought that you might be tired.'

She could have hugged him. 'Oh, how very kind. I was going to catch a tram.'

'That's what Mevrouw thought.' He beamed at her and ushered her into the car. 'You have enjoyed your day, Nurse?'

'Yes, thank you—just roaming round looking at places I'd read about.'

Which was true, she thought suddenly, but she had been escaping too, only she wasn't sure from what; surely not the kind household she was in? Certainly not little Duert. She stopped thinking then and remarked brightly about the charm of the city streets.

She was crossing the hall when Christina opened the drawing-room door and poked her head out. 'There you are,' she declared comfortably. 'If you're not too tired come in for a minute and tell us what kind of a day you've had. The baby's not due for a feed for half an hour and little Duert's being bathed by Nanny— there's nothing for you to do.'

The doctor was there too, and if he noticed Rose's quick glance round the room to see if anyone else was there, he gave no sign. He pulled a chair forward, pulled the bell-rope when his wife suggested that Rose might like a cup of tea, and invited her to tell them about her day.

She enlarged upon the Palace, skipped briskly over the little episode with Mr Werdmer ter Sane and plunged into a detailed account of the visits she had paid to the Begijnhof and Rembrandt's house. 'I loved every minute of it'—she ignored the tiresome exchange with that gentleman—'I wish I'd had more time to potter through the smaller streets . . .'

'Oh, where Sybren lives,' said Christina cheerfully, 'the very best part of town, my dear—you must get him to take you on a stroll—the houses are lovely and all those funny little bridges.' She smiled widely and turned her head as the door opened and he walked in. 'We were just talking about you,' she told him as he bent to kiss her cheek. 'Rose wants to explore the streets in your neighbourhood.'

He straightened and glanced across at Rose, sitting like a poker, her face very pink. 'It's charming certainly,' was all he said, and then, 'I hope you enjoyed your day, Rose?'

'Very much, thank you.' She got up. 'I think I'll go and tuck little Duert up, I dare say Nanny wants to do things for the baby. Thank you for the tea.'

Christina had seen the blush. 'That would be sweet of you. I'll be up presently then he can go to sleep and you'll have plenty of time to change.'

Dr ter Brandt had gone to open the door for her; Mr Werdmer ter Sane was lounging at the window. Rose slid thankfully away.

The moment the door was shut, Christina said, 'Now Sybren, just what happened in the Dam Square? Rose skated over whatever it was, terrified that we would ask questions. Now, give?'

He came and sat down opposite her and Dr ter Brandt sat beside his wife, idly taking her hand in his. 'I asked her not to go poking around the war memorial, oh, a day or so ago. I was driving through this morning and there she was surrounded by a gang of layabouts. I hauled her away and offered to drive her around in the car. She refused, of course.'

Christina said demurely, 'Well, yes. I expect you gave her a piece of your mind . . .'

'I pointed out that she had been foolish.'

'Naturally.' Her voice was still demure and she avoided her husband's eye. 'She wasn't hurt or frightened?' She glanced at his face, blandly calm, hiding his true feelings. 'She made light of it . . .'

'Neither.'

'Oh, good. Perhaps if she goes out again before she leaves us you could spare the time to show her some of the *grachten*.'

'Oh, I would have been delighted, Chrissy, but Mies van Toule is in Amsterdam for a couple of weeks—we haven't seen each other for some time . . .'

'Oh, Mies,' observed Christina brightly, 'she's so pretty—beautiful really, is she here already? You're not going to back out of dining with us?'

He laughed. 'Of course not. And she doesn't get in until tomorrow, I'm going to pick her up at Schiphol.'

Very much later, when Sybren had gone and Rose had gone to bed and the house was quiet, Christina sat brushing her hair while the doctor pottered to and fro, pausing patiently to listen to her comments on the evening.

'They were so awfully polite at dinner,' she mused out loud. 'Darling, I thought that perhaps they were getting a bit interested in each other, didn't you? Sybren is such a dear, he ought to get married and be happy like us. Now he's going to get tangled up with that frightful Mies woman. And Rose—doesn't know she's in love with him, she only knows that he's there, if you see what I mean. Do you suppose she should go back to England before she discovers that? And will he miss her if she does?'

'My love, Sybren is a life-long friend but I would hesitate to guess at his intentions. I agree with you that Rose is probably in love with him and once she's discovered it for herself she will have the greatest

difficulty in hiding it from anyone, and that includes
Sybren. She's very vulnerable, I think, and I would
hate to see her hurt. But Sybren is a dark horse; I
think we'd better leave matters to sort themselves out.'

The next day, being Sunday, it was Nanny's day off
and since Christina was quite her old self again, that
lady consented to be driven to the station to catch her
train to Delft, where she visited her brother. It was
heavenly weather, they took the children into the
garden and sat about chatting and playing with them
while the doctor, who had had a busy week, stretched
out on his beautiful lawn and closed his eyes. Corvinus
brought their coffee out to them and lunch was a
delicious cold meal taken on the patio at the back of
the house. Rose, nicely tired with so much sun, happy
to see little Duert quite well again, and nicely
stimulated by the ter Brandts' light hearted talk,
didn't give Mr Werdmer ter Sane a single thought
until she was on the point of sleep and then it was only
to remember that his name hadn't been mentioned
once all day.

He didn't come for two days and when he did, he
was politely aloof, wanting to know how his little
patient did and nothing more than that. He looked
tired, Rose thought, carefully giving him chapter and
verse and then waiting for any instructions.

They weren't quite what she had expected. 'Well,
Rose, I think we've done what we set out to do. This
young man is as good as new; there's nothing more
you can do for him; Nanny is quite capable of looking
after him and of course Christina is a splendid
mother.'

He was standing quite squarely in front of her,
staring down into her face. She said questioningly,
'When would you like me to leave, Sir?'

'When the ter Brandts can arrange things. I shall look in on the boy whenever I visit. I'll go and see Christina now and drive down to see Duert at the hospital. I must thank you for the real help you have been both to myself and the ter Brandts. I dare say you will be glad to get back to St Bride's. Life has been quiet for you here.'

She looked no higher than his top waistcoat button. 'I've been happy here.'

'I'm glad.' He sounded kind in an impersonal way. 'But you'll be glad to see your family again?'

'Oh, yes.' She couldn't understand why she felt so utterly miserable; she had guessed that she would be leaving very shortly and it had been no surprise. She put out a hand. 'Goodbye, Sir.'

He took her hand and bent to kiss her cheek. He said on a sigh, 'I suppose I shall always be Sir to you, Rose. I wish . . .' He was interrupted by Corvinus coming into the nursery with the information that a Juffrouw van Toule wished to speak to him on the telephone. He went away at once and left Rose wondering who she was. Well, she wasn't likely to know; she picked up little Duert and carried him off for his dinner; there was nothing like work to take one's mind off things.

It was arranged that she should leave in three days' time. She had no need to bother with the details, Dr ter Brandt told her in his calm way; if she would say what time of day she would like to travel he would book her flight and Corvinus would take her to Schiphol. He would also, he told her, telephone Miss Timms and perhaps Rose would like to phone later, and of course she was to phone her aunt as soon as possible.

It was super having everything settled for her; the

ter Brandts were the nicest couple and she thought they were so happy and so sure of each other. She doubted if there were many devoted couples such as they were. Rose paused in the middle of a game of ball with little Duert and allowed herself to day-dream just for a moment—to have a husband who loved you and spent all his life making you happy—it would be wonderful

There was to be a farewell dinner too. 'Such a small return for your kindness and all you have done for us,' declared Christina, 'and look—we're coming over to England in a month or so and we shall come and see you. We're coming on our own, I mean without Nanny—she'll go to her brother's. Duert's a dab hand at changing nappies and listen, Rose, when we get back home again, we want you to come and stay—as our guest, so please say you will. We'll let you know the dates as soon as we can and you can get leave. Please say you will.'

'Oh, I'd love to and thank you for asking me. When will that be?'

'About the end of August. Good, I'm so glad. Now do you want to do any shopping? I'll have little Duert this afternoon and you can go into town. Corvinus can take you and drop you off by the shops, and do take a taxi back.'

So Rose got into the blue dress again and was driven to the main shopping centre and after Corvinus had begged her to be careful and to be sure and get a taxi back, she set off; Noordeinde and Hoogstraat and Lange Voerhout, she explored them all thoroughly, the money she had had no chance to spend burning a hole in her pocket. Finally she found what she wanted; a soft pink crepe dress, very simply cut with a lower neckline than she had ever had before, long sleeves and a calf-length swirling skirt. It was rather more than she had expected to pay but she was feeling reckless and it would do very nicely for the hospital ball next winter. Very satisfied with herself she found six Delft blue coffee cups for her aunt and a silk scarf patterned all over with little Dutch figures for Maggie, and by then it was time to find a taxi and go back to the ter Brandts.

She felt sad on her last day as she packed her case; she had been happy and she had made friends who would remain her friends, not just disappear after a few months. Even if she never saw them after the promised holiday she would know that they were there. As for Mr Werdmer ter Sane, she wouldn't see him again, something which didn't matter at all, she told herself. The feeling of something lost must be because she was sorry to be leaving Holland.

She put little Duert to bed as usual on her last evening, had her usual amicable exchange with Nanny and went to dress. The pink was just as pretty in her own room as it had been in the shop. She pinned up her hair, did her face with care, and then went downstairs. The ter Brandts were in the drawing-room in all the elegance of black tie and silvery chiffon and pearls. 'Oh, very nice,' observed Christina, 'pink suits you and such a pretty dress—where did you get it?'

They swept her along between them and got into the car and somehow between them made her feel confident that she didn't look so bad after all.

They went to the Royal in Woorhout, long established, fashionable and very, very expensive. It was almost full and they had a table in the window with a splendid view of the restaurant around them. Rose, drinking the dry sherry the doctor suggested, looked around her. It was an elegant place and being a

Saturday evening there would be dancing; hence the
black ties and well-dressed women, she supposed. She
ate her way happily through spinach tartlets, chicken à
la King, an enormous confection of ice cream,
chocolate and whipped cream, and drank the champagne in her glass. The evening, as far as she was
concerned, was nothing short of heaven, with the three
of them skimming over any number of subjects in a
light-hearted manner. They were drinking their coffee
when she glanced across the restaurant and saw Mr
Werdmer ter Sane sitting at a table quite close by.
There was a girl with him; a beautiful girl with dark
hair curling around her shoulders, wearing a red dress
with one sleeve and the other shoulder bare. She was
laughing a lot but Mr Werdmer ter Sane wasn't: he
was smiling certainly but he looked, even at that
distance, tired and withdrawn. He looked up and saw
Rose and stared at her, unsmiling, so that she went
very pink. The doctor, happening to glance at her, saw
the look on her face and followed her gaze. His own
remained impassive as he lifted a hand in greeting.
Christina had seen him too by now.

'Sybren's here,' she declared, 'with that Mies girl.'
She caught her husband's eye and went on brightly,
'This place is full tonight, isn't it? It's lovely at
Christmas time, Rose, and at New Year, everyone
wears their very best dress and we dance for hours. Do
you go to many dances in London?'

Rose was forced to answer her; she had got her
blush under control and said in her quiet way, 'Well,
not many—the hospital ball of course, but you see, I'd
need a partner . . .'

The doctor steered the talk away from the pitfalls
ahead. 'Well, will you get a few days leave?' he asked
kindly. 'I did mention to Miss Timms that you hadn't

had anything like the off-duty you're entitled to . . .' He led the conversation back to trivialities and presently when they got up to go called a casual greeting to his friend as they passed their table. Christina greeted him too although she didn't stop and Rose summoned a stiff little smile, puzzling as to why she should feel so shaken at the sight of Mr Werdmer ter Sane; after all they had bidden each other goodbye; it was a pity he hadn't been able to finish what he had been saying when he was called away. And he had looked at her so strangely across the restaurant, as though he was annoyed to see her again. Perhaps he was, she reflected soberly, after all, he had never really liked her as a person even while he had conceded that she was a good nurse.

In the car she said wistfully, 'What a beautiful girl that was . . .'

'With Sybren—very beautiful.' Christina's voice was dry. 'She's to be seen in all the best places . . .'

Saying goodbye the next day was difficult; Rose kissed little Duert's chubby cheek, kissed Christina, was kissed by Dr ter Brandt, bade farewell to Nanny and Sally and got into the car with Corvinus. She felt as though she were leaving some of herself behind, although she told herself robustly that it was no more than an episode which in a few months would be forgotten.

Going through the gate to the plane she told herself that she would start forgetting now, only it wasn't as easy as that; Mr Werdmer ter Sane's face, with that look of annoyance, superimposed itself on her more prosaic thoughts about Miss Timms, St Bride's and the likelihood of holidays.

She had chosen to take a morning flight; she reached St Bride's just as first dinner was over so that several of her friends were crowded into the staff nurses' sitting-room, drinking tea. They fell upon her with gratifying pleasure, plying her with strong tea and a flurry of questions: there was no time to answer them all; they rushed back on duty and she was left to unpack, get her uniform ready for the next morning and then go down to the office to report to Miss Timms.

She was surprised to find that lady unusually gracious. 'You have done well, Staff Nurse,' she was told. 'Both Dr ter Brandt and Mr Werdmer ter Sane have spoken highly of you, indeed Mr Werdmer ter Sane has written to Mr Cresswell in glowing terms and has asked me if I will allow you to make up the off-duty you have had to give up while you were in Holland. I think I can see my way to allowing you four days' leave, Staff Nurse. If you will go and see Sister Cummins and tell her that you will be back on Thursday at one o'clock, there is no reason why you should not be free as from now.'

So Rose flew back to her room, packed a bag once more, phoned her aunt and dashed out to catch a bus to the station. She caught a train to Daventry with minutes to spare and spent the hour-long journey thinking of the things she would do in the next four days.

She was in time to catch the late afternoon bus to Ashby St Ledgers. It was packed and she knew most of the passengers by sight so that they chatted and the short journey passed quickly. The bus was a local one and the driver obligingly stopped whenever anyone wanted to alight, so that progress through the village was slow. They passed the church and the Coach and Horses and the Gate House where the Gunpowder Plot had been hatched, and finally drew to a halt on the corner of a narrow lane. Aunt Millicent's cottage, standing aslant to the village street, looked peaceful and picture-book pretty, its thatched roof in perfect order, its stone walls whitewashed. Rose bade the driver goodbye, picked up her case and went the few yards down the lane to the gate. The path to the cottage was brick with not a weed in sight, and bordered by a lavender hedge along its entire length. There was a wide stretch of grass to one side of the cottage leading to the kitchen garden at the back and Rose had no doubt that the beans and peas and potatoes were growing in an orderly manner; they wouldn't dare to do otherwise under Aunt Millicent's eye.

She was suddenly happy and ran up the path to the door and pushed it wide open. 'I'm here, Aunt Millicent—Maggie . . .'

Both ladies came into the narrow hall to welcome her, each in her own fashion. 'Nice to see you,' said her aunt. 'You look tired, my dear, I'm glad they let you come home . . .'

Rose hugged her, it was nice to hear Aunt Millicent say that; she felt a sudden urge to burst into tears, luckily prevented by Maggie's urgent, 'Now you sit down this minute, the pair of you. I'll bring a nice tray of tea and you can sit for half an hour. Worn to the socket you must be—all very well that man praising you to the skies, a lot of good that does if a body's worn to a thread.'

She bustled away to the kitchen and Rose asked, 'What man? And do I look so awful?'

'Tired—I said so,' observed Miss Curtis. 'Mister Werdmer ter Sane wrote to me—he seemed very impressed with your work; said you'd been invaluable and regretted the loss of your free time. I had a

charming letter from Mevrouw ter Brandt too.' She
smiled as they sat down opposite each other in the
low-ceilinged room. 'You've earned your holiday,
Rose.'

Maggie came in with the tea then and since she was
almost one of the family, she fetched a cup for herself
and listened while Rose told them the more interesting
bits about her stay in Amsterdam and The Hague.

Presently she went away, albeit reluctantly, to see
about supper and Rose sat back in the shabby
armchair that was so comfortable, nicely filled with tea
and several slices of Maggie's lardy cake.

'Were you homesick?' asked her aunt.

'No I didn't have time for that and by the time I did
everyone was so nice that I felt almost at home. The
ter Brandts were so kind . . .'

'And Mr Werdmer ter Sane?'

'Kind?' She thought about it. 'Well, yes in a way.
You see, I was the nurse there to do as he asked; I
don't really think that he thought of me as a person, if
you see what I mean.'

'Married?' Aunt Millicent's voice was casual.

'No, but he's got a girl friend, I don't know if they
are engaged yet—she'd been away but she came back
to Amsterdam while I was there, she's like a fashion-
plate—very, very pretty and not a hair out of place and
when I saw her she was wearing a way-out dress—
everyone was looking at her.'

Aunt Millicent gave a snort. 'What does she do for a
living?'

'Do? Oh Aunt Millicent, girls like her don't work. I
expect she has loads of money, anyway.'

'There's no accounting for tastes,' observed Miss
Curtis, a remark which might have meant anything.

The weather was heavenly; Rose, in a rather faded

cotton dress which had luckily been found in a
cupboard in her bedroom, gardened under her aunt's
stern guidance, helped around the house, and strolled
through the lanes and fields round the village. Days
had never gone so fast, the idea of St Bride's and the
narrow busy streets round the hospital filled her with
a longing to stay where she was, but at least, she told
herself, she would be coming back again; the cottage
would still be there for years to come and she was sure
of a welcome. It was a pity she felt so unsettled
though; she tried to get to the bottom of it as she hung
out the sheets for Maggie before breakfast on her last
day. She had almost finished when the gate creaked.

She whipped round to see who it was, struck with
devastatingly final clarity by the knowledge that just
for a split second she had hoped that it was Mr
Werdmer ter Sane. Of course, it wasn't; Henry, the
boy from the village shop, was clomping up the path
with the day's news. He shouted a cheerful greeting
and she answered him in a rather wispy voice, shocked
at her own thoughts. She pegged the last sheet and
then stood looking at it. All these days she had been
wanting to see him again only she hadn't admitted it,
even to herself. It was extremely foolish of her to wish
it; even if they did meet again no good would come of
it. Just for a moment common sense fled from her
sensible head and day-dreams took over; supposing,
just supposing, they were to meet again and he was
glad to see her; looked at her as he had looked at the
beautiful Mies, told her that he had missed her. Rose
stood in the bright morning sunshine, lost in her
dream.

It only lasted a minute or two; she picked up the
washing-basket and started back to the kitchen door.
'You are daft, Rose,' she muttered, 'you think you've

fallen in love with him; ten to one if you met him again you'd turn and run.' A lie if ever there was one.

She hated leaving the next morning, the village lay peaceful under warm sunshine and lovely blue skies, it didn't seem possible that she was in the same world when she got out of the taxi at St Bride's; the sun wasn't warm, it was hot, piercing the motionless air laden with petrol fumes, even the blue sky seemed to have shrunk. Rose went over to the nurses' home and unpacked and got into her uniform and went down to dinner in the canteen. All her friends were there and she cheered up under the warmth of their greetings, and regaled her with the latest hospital gossip. But half way through a particularly spicy titbit about the new surgical houseman and Mr Cresswell, Sadie stopped and said, 'Rose, you're not with us—what's the matter? You're *distraite*—not just fed up at coming back.' She started to say something else but the look on Rose's face stopped her. She finished lamely, 'Oh, well, I dare say you are hating it all—it's beastly coming back ... Let's all get together over a pot of tea after we're off duty and then we can hear all about Holland.'

Rose cast her a thankful look. 'Okay, Maggie gave me a super cake, we can have that with the tea.'

Sister Cummins was glad to see her back and there were still several small patients left from before Rose had gone to Holland. There were a lot of new little faces too and she plunged straight into the busy routine. Half way through the afternoon Miss Timms sent for her.

'You enjoyed your leave, Staff Nurse?' she wanted to know.

Rose said that yes, she had, thank you.

'I am told,' said Miss Timms with dignified

geniality, 'by Dr ter Brandt, that he and his wife wish you to pay them a visit later in the summer. This may cause some inconvenience on Sister Cummins' ward but I feel that an effort must be made to accede to his request. You will let Sister Cummins know the date as soon as possible, Staff Nurse, so that things may be arranged satisfactorily.'

She nodded her rigidly coiffed head and Rose made a speedy exit before Miss Timms could have second thoughts. The ter Brandts weren't coming to England for at least a month and they had asked her to go after that . . . a lot could happen in that time and Miss Timms could change her mind.

The afternoon and evening seemed endless but at last she was off duty, her shoes off, comfortably dressing-gowned, cutting Maggie's cake while mugs of tea were handed round. The cake eaten, and mugs refilled, someone asked: 'Well, what happened in Amsterdam or wherever it was Rose? Did you meet anyone groovy? What were the housemen like? And what about that super specimen who came over here to fetch you?'

'Mister Werdmer ter Sane,' said Rose; she was amazed how calm and indifferent her voice sounded while her heart thumped and thudded at the mere mention of his name. 'Yes, of course, I saw him—every day at first—little Duert was very ill and no one quite knew what would happen.'

'Did he take you out?'

'Heavens no. I was the nurse, remember. Besides he's got a steady—a simply ravishing girl . . .'

It was Sadie who said in a disappointed voice: 'Oh, has he? I suppose he'd forgotten all about me—us, calling at his house?'

'No, as a matter of fact, he hadn't—he spoke of

you—he certainly hadn't forgotten you, Sadie.'

There was a burst of laughter. 'Good old Sadie, competing with the Dutch glamour girl.' A voice from the back cried, 'You should have gone instead of Rose.' Everyone laughed again, but it was kind laughter; they all liked Rose. They were a little taken aback at her fervent, 'Oh, I wish you had, Sadie.' She wouldn't have fallen in love with him then, would she? She would have remained heart-whole, content to carve a career for herself in the nursing world, her simple sensible head clear of silly dreams about a handsome, aloof Dutchman, who she was pretty certain had already forgotten all about her.

But the ter Brandts hadn't forgotten her; the even balance of her busy days was disturbed by a letter from Christina ter Brandt; they had decided to come to England earlier than they had planned; they would be staying in London for a few days, and would she come to see them? Dinner, suggested Christina, or failing a free evening, lunch and she would phone as soon as they arrived during the following week, so that they could plan something. The baby flourished and little Duert was as good as new and they all sent their love, and that included Nanny, Corvinus and Sally. There was not one word about Sybren Werdmer ter Sane.

Rose wrote back cautiously: she would love to see them all again but it depended on whether she was free; Miss Timms had already offered her leave when she wanted it and she wasn't going to spoil her chances for that. It was madness, she told herself over and over again, to see Mr Werdmer ter Sane again, but nothing was going to stop her. She was sensible enough to know that it would do her no good; the quicker she forgot about him the better, only she was finding it

singularly difficult to shake him off. Going round the
ward, taking temperatures, adjusting drips, feeding
the small creatures who couldn't for the time being,
feed themselves, his face rose before her eyes a dozen
times a day. It was most inconvenient, and such a
waste of time, he would have consigned her to
oblivion.

He might have wished to do so, but unwillingly
enough, he had thought of her a good deal on a
number of occasions. Why, he asked himself irritably,
should a small plain girl, unfashionable as to dress and
lacking in witty conversation, remain so persistently in
his head to annoy him? And why, in heaven's name,
did he cancel everything when Mr Cresswell phoned
him and asked him if he would be good enough to co-
operate with him on a particularly tricky operation at
St Bride's and accept with alacrity?!

He arrived at St Bride's quite early in the morning
and joined Mr Creswell there, and the first person he
saw, probably because he was looking for her, was
Rose.

She had not known that he was coming; Sister
Cummins had told her that the toddler with cancer of
the leg was to be operated upon by Mr Cresswell but
she hadn't said a word about anyone else taking part in
it. Rose knew that it was a difficult operation; very few
had been attempted so far but if it were successful it
should be a miraculous recovery for the child. Rose,
who had been specialing the little girl, had just bathed
and fed her when the two surgeons arrived. Mr
Cresswell's 'Good morning Rose' was genial, Mr
Werdmer ter Sane gave her a tight-lipped greeting
which instantly quenched the glow of delight which
had enveloped her at the sight of him. She muttered
something in reply, aware that she must appear

gauche, the very last thing that she would wish to be, so that at once she became the very epitome of professional perfection, answering Mr Cresswell's questions in a colourless and correct voice, which made him exclaim, 'Good God, Rose, have you swallowed the poker?' A remark which brought her down from the heights of correctness to her usual sensible manner. She even replied to several of Mr Werdmer ter Sane's civil remarks in her usual calm manner and sat on the side of the cot with the toddler on her lap while they gently examined her. Mr Werdmer ter Sane had to bend very close so that his handsome features were only inches away and she could see the grey hair which grew as thickly as the fair. She closed her eyes so as not to see it, and he, looking up for a moment, stared at her face; she might not be pretty but the dark lashes sweeping her cheeks were some of the longest and curliest he had ever seen. He frowned quite fiercely so that when she opened them again it was to meet his beetling brows. She met his look with a calm she didn't feel; he disliked her even more than she had thought. No, dislike wasn't the word, indifferent described the stare he had given her.

They would operate in two days' time; there were tests to be carried out first and the parents had to be told of the risks and the chance of success. 'And you will bring the child to theatre,' said Mr Cresswell, 'and special her afterwards, that'll knock your off-duty for six, but you must be used to that by now, Rose. I'll see Sister Cummins when she comes on duty and get things fixed up. We'll operate at eight o'clock and it'll take all of seven hours—perhaps more. What do you say, Sybren?'

'Seven with luck on our side.'

The two men wandered off down the ward, and Rose, nicely thoughtful of their needs, sent the third-year student nurse after them to see that they had the coffee they would almost certainly expect. It had been a shock seeing Mr Werdmer ter Sane again but she had no doubt that by the time they met again in theatre she would have come to terms with the situation. Two days would be ample time in which to pull herself together.

CHAPTER FIVE

ROSE worked very hard at getting herself into a rational frame of mind, helped considerably by not seeing Mr Werdmer ter Sane during the next two days. He came on to the ward but always while she was off-duty, so that she received his and Mr Cresswell's instructions through Sister Cummins. But while she was on duty at least she had little time to think about him, the toddler was ill, would indeed die if the operation wasn't successful, and over and above that, there were other ill children in the ward in need of constant attention. The student nurses worked hard but there were some treatments they weren't able to do so that Rose and Sister Cummins had more than enough on their hands. On the evening before the operation Sister Cummins, giving the report to Rose before she went off-duty for the evening, remarked that she would be glad when it was all over. 'I know we cope with all kinds of surgery, but this is going to be an all-day affair and even after that, Shirley will need to be specialed ... I know Mr Cresswell wants you to do that, but leaves us very short-handed.' She frowned. 'I did suggest to Mr Werdmer ter Sane that the specialing could be done by a third-year nurse, even a qualified nurse from another ward if I could borrow one, but he was adamant. You or no one. Well, I can't blame him, you're a good nurse and it'll be a feather in our caps—yours especially, if Shirley pulls through.' She went to the office door on her way off duty. 'Your time off may have to be shelved for a day or two but you know that, don't you, Staff? I'll see it's made up to you.'

There were two student nurses on with Rose until the night staff arrived. They went softly round the ward, settled the little ones for the night and she checked dressings and the very ill children. Shirley was already in a side ward and asleep, too young to bother about what was to happen next and too ill to mind. Rose was taking her temperature when Mr Werdmer ter Sane came quietly in.

Rose finished what she was doing, aware that her heart was behaving badly again and thankful that in the darkened ward he couldn't see her face.

His 'Hullo, Rose', was quiet and devoid of expression. She murmured back at him, fastened the cot side soundlessly and waited for him to speak.

She had no idea what he was going to say and was taken aback when he said, 'Christina and Duert send their love and so does little Duert. You know they are coming over soon?' And at her surprised nod, 'I'm to tell you that Christina will phone you at the end of the week. She knows about Shirley and realises that you won't be free until then.'

Rose said, 'Oh, yes. Well . . .' and found her head empty of words. The two days hadn't been enough, she doubted very much if two years would be enough either, even two hundred.

Mr Werdmer ter Sane eyed her narrowly across the cot. Even in the dim light she looked rather plain for she was very tired and hungry for her supper. The thought passed through his mind that his strange wish to see her again must have been born of imagination, she was just about the least glamorous girl he had ever set eyes on. 'Well, shall we go over your instructions for tomorrow?' he asked briskly, amazed that he had had some vague idea of inviting her out to supper.

They parted presently with polite good nights, he to go to the consultants' room to have a final brief talk with Mr Cresswell and his registrar, and she to the office where the night staff were waiting impatiently for the report. It took longer than usual for there were all the extra instructions for Shirley's pre-op treatment. By the time Rose got to the canteen, suppers were over and the counter was bare. The night cook and her companions in the kitchen were getting the night nurses' midnight meal ready. Rose went over to her room and then joined her friends in Sadie's room to drink tea and eat biscuits. But she was still hungry. There was a coffee stall down the street from the hospital where one could buy hot baked potatoes and pies. She fetched her purse and nipped out of a side door, bent on buying hot poatoes for herself and various of her friends. It was just unfortunate that on her return she should run full tilt into Mr Werdmer ter Sane crossing the forecourt to his car. He stood her upright and looked at the bag of potatoes she was clasping with both hands, and although he hadn't said a word she felt compelled to speak. 'So sorry, Sir—I was in a hurry . . .'

'Supper?'

'Yes, I was too late for the canteen.' She gave him a disconcertingly clear look from her brown eyes and slipped past him and through the side door again. Mr Werdmer ter Sane, bidden to dine with friends at the Savoy, angrily spurned the feeling of positively tender compassion which seized him. The ridiculous thought that he would like to see her smile, hear her laugh, take the pins out of her severe bun of hair and buy her more flowers than she could hold in her arms, received the same severe treatment.

He muttered a few telling phrases in his own language, got into his car and drove to his hotel to change for the dinner party. The friends he was dining with had a charming daughter, pretty and witty and always dressed in the forefront of fashion. Undoubtedly she would dispel the extraordinary ideas he had; he had known her for some time and was aware, without conceit, that she would marry him if he asked her. He didn't love her and he was sure that she didn't love him, but they had similar interests and he had the money which she found essential to her way of life. He had come to the conclusion some years ago that there was to be no ideal woman for him; for one thing, he wasn't sure what she would be like.

The dinner party was delightful, Charmian, the daughter, wittier and prettier than ever, the food delicious. Half way through the *boeuf bourguignon*, he found himself wishing that he was eating baked potatoes with Rose. The thought merely made him more attentive to Charmian, nonetheless he left early with the pretext that he was operating early the next morning.

Rose, gobbling her potato with a healthy appetite, listened to the chatter around her without hearing it. She was thinking lovingly of Mr Werdmer ter Sane, blissfully aware that she would see him for hours on end the next day even though they wouldn't exchange a word. But just to be there, watching him operate was something she recognised as a bonus. He would go back to Holland almost at once, she supposed, for he was a busy man but in the meantime she would see him again. It was a pity that they had met on her way back with the potatoes ... She was roused from her

thoughts by someone wanting to know if she intended
to apply for the post of junior night sister which was
unexpectedly vacant at the end of the month. No one
seemed to want it—night duty was never popular, but
as Sadie pointed out, it was a useful stepping off
ground for a day sister's post if one became vacant.
'Not that I want it,' said Sadie, tossing her curls, 'I
dare say we'll get married next year. Rose, you are
going to be a bridesmaid so don't go deciding on any
holidays until I know the date.'

Rose went on duty early so that she could do all the
last-minute chores for Shirley before she took the
child to the theatre. The small leg had already been
prepped; she sat the drowsy child on her lap and tied
the theatre gown down her back, and sat quietly then
with Shirley cuddled up to her own theatre gown.
Shirley opened a sleepy eye and Rose beamed down at
her. 'Beautiful moppet,' she said softly, 'you'll grow
up to be a gorgeous princess and a handsome prince
will come along and marry you and you'll be happy
ever after and your leg will never hurt again, so just
you close that eye and go to sleep again and when you
wake up I'll be here to tell you more about that
prince.'

Mr Werdmer ter Sane, on the ward earlier than
expected, paused in the doorway and listened to
Rose's soft voice, staring at her small straight back and
neat head crowned by the stiffly frilled cap the staff
nurses wore. He was sure, without conceit, that if any
one could save Shirley's leg, he could, at the same time
he was glad that Rose would be there in theatre; she
was just as sure as he was and two determined people
were so much better than one. He retreated
soundlessly and then retraced his steps, and made just
enough noise for her to hear him come.

His 'Good morning, Rose', was pleasantly civil, he
bent over Shirley for a moment, remarked that he
would see them in the theatre very shortly, suggested
that Rose should carry the child there instead of using
the usual trolley, and went away again.

Shirley didn't rouse as Rose wrapped her in a
blanket and carried her the short journey to the theatre
wing. The anaesthetist grunted at her as she laid the
child carefully down; he was a dour Scot who had a
marvellous way with children but wasted few words
on anyone else. Rose said good morning cheerfully in
answer to the grunt and began her various duties
without fuss. She liked theatre and the surgeons liked
to have her there; she was quiet and did what she was
told at once and had a tremendous capacity for staying
on her feet for hours at a stretch. Mr Cresswell,
coming in to take a look, said: 'Hullo Rose, ready
for a hard day's work, I hope,' and went away again
and presently they were all in theatre, ready to
start.

Mr Werdmer ter Sane was operating; nobody had
attempted that particular surgery in England, although
he had had success with two cases in Vienna, so that
he would take the lead, inaugurating a new technique
which Mr Cresswell would continue with further
cases. It was daring, but Shirley was going to die if
nothing was done and the previous patients were
doing well. He bent his great height over the table and
started his work.

It was long, tedious and painstaking work; the two
men with the registrar and one of the house surgeons
assisting, cut, sawed, dissected, trimmed, pinned and
plated with controlled patience, muttering to each
other from time to time, pausing momentarily to
assess their work. Theatre Sister, known throughout

the hospital as Clean Kate because of her obsessive
cleanliness, stood stolidly passing instruments and
swabs for the almost six hours which the operation
took, although the scrubbed staff nurse backing her up
was replaced half way through by a second. The
theatre nurses did the same, but Rose stayed where
she was by the anaesthetist, with a short break for a
cup of coffee towards midday. The operation was
going well; when she wasn't attending to the
anaesthetist's wants, Rose watched Mr Werdmer ter
Sane's large hands fitting things together with the
precision of a skilled needlewoman making a patchwork
quilt. She found it fascinating, hardly noticing the
hours slipping away, until at length he and Mr
Cresswell stood back leaving the registrar to the final
stitching. After a moment they stripped off their
gloves, thanked everyone there for their help and left
the theatre. Rose pictured them swallowing hot coffee
and devouring sandwiches in Sister's office; they must
be famished, and come to think of it she was famished
too.

It was another hour before she was relieved for
her own meal. First there was Shirley to escort to
intensive care where she would remain for the rest
of the day and the following night and in the
morning she would be transferred back into Rose's
care.

Midday dinner had been cleared away for an hour
or more by the time she got to the canteen but cold
meat and pickles and a bowl of lettuce had been left
for those who had been in theatre. Rose ate this
sustaining but unexciting meal in the company of
the theatre staff and then went back to the ward,
for there were still two hours of duty to get
through.

Not that she had time to grumble about that; the room in which Shirley was to be nursed had to be prepared, the equipment, and there was a lot of it, tested and put in place, the panic trolley positioned so that it could be got at in seconds, and when Rose was at last satisfied that everything was as it should be, there were a couple of dressings to do on the ward before Sister Cummins came on duty for the evening. By the time she had given the report, gone over the operation in detail, conned the off-duty with her so that there would be sufficient staff to cover the next day, it was half past five.

Too late for tea and too early for supper. She went to her room, had a shower and got into a cotton dress, tied her hair back and looked at her clock. There was still almost an hour before the canteen would be open and she was too tired to get on a bus and go to one of the cheaper restaurants in Oxford Street. She lolled out of the window; it was such a lovely evening that even the shabby roofs and chimney pots around the hospital looked different. Then someone tapped on the door and she said 'Come in' without looking round. 'Don't ask me to go out,' she began and saw that it was the home warden, a middle-aged bony lady of uncertain age who gave the strong impression of disapproving of anyone under the age of forty. She said now in a severe voice, 'There's someone in the visitor's room to see you.'

'Not me,' said Rose instantly, 'I don't know anyone . . . I expect it's Staff Nurse Chumley you want, she's got dozens of boy friends.'

The warden gave her a nasty look. 'I don't make mistakes in names,' she observed chillingly. 'Staff Nurse Comely I was told to fetch, and that's what I'm doing.'

'Do you know who it is?'

'No, I do not. Nor is it my business to ask.' She turned such a basilisk stare upon Rose that she said, 'Oh, well I suppose I'd better go down.'

She skipped past the warden who warned, 'Not the Sister's lift, Staff Nurse.'

So of course Rose felt compelled to do exactly what she was told not to do.

The visitor's room had been designed to damp any ardour felt by the nurses' men friends, it smelled of polish and the linoleum floor struck chill into their hearts as well as their feet. The chairs were tubular steel and imitation leather and gave no comfort to the sitter. There was a plain wooden table in the exact centre with a rubber plant upon it.

Rose opened the door slowly, wondering who she would see. The sight of Mr Werdmer ter Sane sitting on the table with the rubber plant was rather more than she had expected. Her 'Oh, heavens above, it's you,' was spontaneous if unflattering. She paused inside the door and he got to his feet making the small room even smaller.

'In person, Rose, We've had a hard day; I wondered if we might enjoy one of your high teas together?'

She goggled at him. 'High tea?' she repeated unnecessarily. 'They don't have high tea in the sort of restaurant you'd go to.'

'Something which must be remedied. The porter tells me that there's a place called Lyons Corner House opposite Charing Cross station. I don't know about you but I'm famished.'

She stayed where she was, her hand still on the door knob. 'Why do you want to take me?' she asked. 'There's Sadie ... I know she's off this evening.'

He said patiently, 'That was quite a job we did

today, I'd like to mull it over with someone who
knows what I'm talking about.'

She nodded her head, it wasn't exactly a flattering
reason and it didn't do much for her ego, but she
understood how he felt.

'Yes, it's not fashionable but the food's good and
they don't rush you.'

'Let's go then?'

She hesitated. 'My hair—and I haven't got my
purse.'

'The hair's fine.' Like a small girl's, he thought,
very clean and shining. 'And you won't need a purse,
will you? I've a handkerchief with me and small
change.' He added kindly, 'Your face doesn't need any
fussing over.'

She didn't answer, well aware that no amount of
fussing would turn her into a beauty. 'Then I'm
ready,' she told him quietly.

He ignored his car in the park. 'Nowhere to leave
it,' he explained, 'we can take a taxi.'

Which they did, not speaking much as they were
driven from the East End along the Commercial Road
and Fleet Street and into the Strand. The Corner
House looked welcoming as they stood looking at it
from the pavement.

'It's not in the least like that marvellous place the
ter Brandts took me to,' observed Rose doubtfully.

He didn't answer her, but swept her inside and sat
her down at a table for two in the window, and then
handed her the menu and said, 'Now, choose our high
tea.'

The place was brightly lit even though it was barely
dusk and the smell of food was delicious. Besides it
was almost full of customers, eating and drinking and
talking and laughing. Rose was aware that it was

hardly her companion's scene but since he wanted high tea he was going to get it.

'Tea for two,' she told him, 'a pot of tea—bacon and egg and sausages and tomatoes, toast and butter, jam and a plate of cakes,' She cast a quick look at him but not a muscle of his face moved. 'Scottish high tea has scones, baps and soda bread,' she explained.

'It sounds delightful but we'll make do with the English version, shall we?' And when the waitress arrived he ordered everything she had suggested, and when the tray of food arrived he ate it with an enjoyment which was much enhanced by the sight of Rose, obviously enjoying every mouthful. And if he would have liked something else to drink other than the strong tea he was offered he didn't say so, and throughout the meal he talked of this and that and in such an undemanding way, and it wasn't until Rose had polished off a Danish pastry and poured the last of the tea, that he spoke of the operation that day. He hadn't meant to do more than make some light reference to it although he had told her otherwise, but that, he had to admit, had been because he wanted an excuse to take her out. A meal at Lyons was hardly his idea of taking a girl out, but then Rose wasn't his kind of girl. He couldn't call to mind any of his girl friends who would have listened to him boring on about pins and plates and shortening of the bone. But Rose wasn't bored. What was more, she asked sensible questions and listened to the answers. He paused presently. 'Am I boring you?'

She gave him the clear look he found so disquieting. 'No, I wanted to ask all sorts of questions in the theatre. It was a splendid operation, the first of many I hope. Just think, Shirley will grow up and be able to dance and run . . .'

'Her leg will be almost three inches shorter.'

'It's surely possible to get a special shoe. And she'll be alive . . .'

'You don't think that will prevent her from marrying?'

'Why ever should it? If someone falls in love with her—and she's going to grow into a very pretty girl, you know—do you suppose he'll care about that? If he loves her? Look at the thousands of plain girls who get married . . .' She stopped and the colour rushed into her face. But she didn't look away.

'Beauty is in the eye of the beholder,' his voice was very kind but not in the least pitying. 'And I don't believe that there is a living soul who is completely plain. A girl with a plain face may have beautiful legs or a lovely body or magnificent eyes, sometimes all three. Most fortunately, as you observed, Shirley is a pretty child and will grow into a pretty woman, probably clever enough to know how to conceal her damaged leg to her best advantage.'

'You've given her that chance.'

'Yes, but I couldn't have done that without help from other people, you for one.' He smiled suddenly and her heart rocked. 'Shall we have another pot of tea?'

With the coming of the fresh pot came fresh conversation. She wasn't quite sure how it had all started, but she found herself telling him about her stepmother and Aunt Millicent and Maggie, only at the last minute did she remember not to let him know where Aunt Millicent lived. She had no idea why she wanted to keep that a secret but it seemed important that she should. And presently their talk swung back to St Bride's which reminded Rose to say, 'Sadie hopes she'll see you again before you go away. She's one of the nicest people I know—we've been friends from the first day we started training.'

'A charming girl,' was all he was going to say. 'I shall be in London for a few more days, just to see Shirley turn the corner and at the same time look up a few old friends.'

'I expect you have a great many?' Rose put down her cup. 'Would you mind if we went back now? I'm on duty at half past seven tomorrow morning.'

He lifted a finger for the bill. 'Until when?'

'Oh, just for a couple of days I'll be on all day except when I go to a meal. It's much better if there are just two of us on a special case like Shirley.'

They went out into the summer evening and he hailed a taxi. 'I hope you will be free to spend some time with Christina and Duert.'

'Oh, I expect so. It will be nice to see little Duert and the baby.'

She sat rather primly beside him and he glanced sideways at her. She was tired now and a little pale, her mane of hair looked too heavy for her neck. Her hands, too, lay neatly clasped in her cotton lap. She turned her head suddenly, her lovely eyes thoughtful. 'Will you tell me why you asked me to come out with you? I'm not your sort of a companion, am I? And I don't suppose you have ever been inside a Lyons before or eaten high tea?'

He answered her slowly, 'I'm not sure myself, Rose. Shall we put it down to a sudden urge to do something different? I've enjoyed our evening.'

She mused sadly that probably he thought of her and a place like Lyons Corner House in the same breath; she was quite sure that the beautiful girl she had seen him with would never have gone there. For that matter, he would never have suggested it in the first place. When the taxi stopped she thanked him again, but he got out with her. 'I'm going to see Shirley,' he told her and waved away her repeated thanks. 'A pleasure, Rose.' He looked down at her. 'You're tired, aren't you?'

She said that yes, she was; she was unhappy too, but that was her secret.

She saw him often enough during the next few days; he came several times a day to take a look at Shirley, sometimes with Mr Cresswell, sometimes by himself, and he had nothing to say to her other than matters concerned with the toddler. And on the third day he paused long enough to say: 'She'll do. Thank you, Rose.'

Mr Cresswell came alone or with his registrar after that and Rose tried very hard to believe that she didn't mind not seeing Mr Werdmer ter Sane again. After all, she told herself sensibly, no good would come of meeting him. He had been kind, taking her out to a meal, but then he would be kind to a stray dog or an old lady who had fallen down in the street. She was aware that a good doctor or surgeon had a degree of compassion tucked away out of sight which perhaps the ordinary man in the street didn't possess. She had no wish to be pitied, she told herself firmly, and redoubled her efforts to get small Shirley on to the road to recovery again.

It was little short of a miracle that the child should make such a splendid recovery for the operation had been a severe one. Of course there would be frequent check-ups to make sure that there were no secondaries, and it would be some weeks before she would take her first few steps, but the leg—its sound parts neatly put together again, the cancer cut away—encased in plaster, was healing just as it should.

It was almost a week before Rose heard from Christina. They were in London, staying at the Connaught Hotel and would Rose have dinner with them one evening soon? She would phone, said Christina's note and Rose could tell her on which evening she would be free.

Sister Cummins allowed her a half-day and the promise of a long week-end at the end of the following week; she added graciously that since Rose had been so cooperative about her off-duty during the last few days she might choose which evening she would like. So she phoned Christina and agreed to have dinner with them in two days' time, which gave her the time to wash her hair and do her nails and make sure that the crepe dress she so seldom had the opportunity to wear was quite pristine.

She would be fetched, Christina had said, and it was nice to find Duert ter Brandt waiting for her in his own car when she got to the hospital entrance. He greeted her with his usual calm, gave her news of his small son, enlarged on the beauty of his little daughter and observed that both he and Christina were delighted to have the chance to see her again. And by then they were at the hotel.

'We're on the first floor,' explained the doctor. 'We need to spread ourselves as the children are with us.'

Rose wasn't quite prepared for the delightful sitting-room into which she was ushered. She glanced round her at its comfort; her experience of hotels was slight but it seemed to her to be the height of luxury. There were doors on either side, one of which was opened as they went in and Christina came hurrying in, and behind her, not hurrying at all, Mr Werdmer ter Sane. The last person she had expected to see.

Christina greeted her warmly and hugged her. 'How

lovely to see you, Rose,' she exclaimed, 'and what a pretty dress.' She nodded carelessly in Mr Werdmer ter Sane's direction, 'Sybren's here too—just to cast an eye on little Duert, you know.'

Rose said 'Hullo,' in a calm little voice while her heart thudded against her ribs. Surely he could have done that while they were in Holland? After all he only lived half an hour's drive away. Why come to London?

Christina answered her unspoken thought. 'It gives him a chance to enjoy the bright lights. Come and see the children . . .' She whisked Rose away to admire them in their respective cots. 'I do love Nanny,' confided Christina, 'but it's rather fun to have them all to ourselves and Duert is so good with them. Of course we couldn't do that in The Hague, Duert's days are so busy and it's quite a large house to manage.' She smiled at Rose. 'Will you come and spend a week with us soon? Sybren says he had to come over here again in two weeks' time and he'll give you a lift. Do say you'll come?'

Rose was bending over the baby's cot. 'I'd love to come; I'll have to see if I can get a week off. But there's no need for Mr Werdmer ter Sane to give me a lift; I can get a plane so easily.'

Christina gave her a quick glance. 'Yes, of course, but let us know when you can come, won't you? We shan't be going back home for ten days—you can fix something up before then?'

'Oh, yes. Will you be here—in London?'

'We're going to spend a day or two with friends of Duert's but not until next week.' She tucked her small son in cosily. 'Doesn't he look sweet? I'll never thank you enough, Rose.'

Rose said gruffly: 'My goodness, I didn't do much, it was Mr Werdmer der Sane . . .'

'Isn't his name a mouthful, why don't you call him Sybren?'

'Well . . . I don't know him very well and anyway I don't think he'd like it.'

To which Christina said nothing but led the way back to the sitting room where they were given drinks and were absorbed immediately into undemanding conversation.

Presently the floor waiter brought dinner and they sat around the table with its snowy cloth and gleaming glass and cutlery and ate a delicious meal in a leisurely fashion. Rose, very conscious of Sybren sitting opposite her, was quite unaware of what she ate.

It was a warm evening; they had their coffee on the balcony outside the sitting-room, and London, veiled in the summer twilight, looked lovely and mysterious too. Well, amended Rose to herself, that particular bit of London; she doubted if the streets round St Bride's could look lovely even if one employed the liveliest of imaginations. Which reminded her that it was time she left. She caught Christina's eye. 'If you don't mind, I must go—I'm on duty early in the morning . . .' She added: 'It's been a lovely evening, thank you . . .'

'We've enjoyed having you, Rose.' It was Dr ter Brandt who spoke. 'Before you go will you promise to phone us here and tell us when you can come and see us?'

'Yes, of course. I'll see about it tomorrow, and thank you for asking me.' They were all on their feet and Sybren said, 'I'll run you back.'

'No—no, there's no need, I can get a taxi.' Rose's pleasant voice was so sharp that they all looked at her. It was Sybren who said easily, 'I've not had a chance to ask you about Shirley—I thought you might bring me up to date on the way back to St Bride's.'

Rose blushed and felt foolish. 'Of course—I'm sorry. But I didn't want to break up your party—you must want to talk.'

Christina said gently, 'Sybren's spending the night here; we've all the time in the world to talk. It's been a lovely evening and don't forget to let us know when you can get that week off.' She put an arm round Rose and kissed her lightly and her husband did the same while Sybren looked on with an expressionless face. Perhaps he'll kiss me when we say goodbye, thought Rose, and went a very bright pink at the idea, unaware that her face was an open book to be read by anyone who cared to look. And Sybren was looking.

There wasn't a great deal of traffic and at first the streets were pleasant; well lit, the great houses on either side standing in silent dignity, but as they neared St Bride's the houses became small and cramped, and so did the streets, with discarded Coca Cola tins and greasy newspapers from chip suppers blowing to and fro.

'Another world, isn't it?' observed Mr Werdmer ter Sane.

Rose said that yes it was, and in more ways than one, she added silently. She had enjoyed every minute of her evening, but it had been like peering through an open door at delights which could never be hers. As he drew up in the courtyard she put her hand on the door, suddenly anxious to be gone, but he leaned across her and covered her hand in his. 'No, wait, Rose, what's the matter?'

She was surprised so that she could only mutter, 'Matter?' in a stupid fashion.

'That's what I said. You are unhappy, hiding it nicely but underneath that serene face you are on the boil, why?'

She answered him in a hurry. 'Oh, there is nothing. I'm tired; Shirley's been a full-time job. You wanted to know about her; she is doing marvellously; her mother and father . . .'

He interrupted her. 'Yes, I know. I've had a talk with them. She'll do very well, I think although we can't know for certain just yet.'

She turned to look at him then. 'But you wanted to know about her—you know already—there was no need . . .'

'None at all,' he told her coolly, 'but you would have dug in your toes about coming back with me, wouldn't you?'

'Yes.' It sounded bald, but she couldn't think of anything further to say. He took his hand away abruptly. She heard him sigh as he got out and went round the bonnet to open her door. Anxious to make amends she said timidly, 'It was nice meeting you again . . .'

'Nice, nice? There was nothing nice about it.' He sounded mocking and his laugh held no amusement. 'It's a great pity . . .' He didn't go on and when she looked up at him he said quietly, 'Good night. Rose.'

An unhappy ending to a happy evening and the quicker she took herself in hand the better. A fruitless task which cost her almost all of a night's sleep.

She would have given a great deal not to have gone on duty in the morning; Mr Werdmer ter Sane would most certainly come to inspect Shirley's leg. Which he did, while she was at her dinner. She wasn't sure whether to be glad or sorry about it when she got back to Shirley, but the wish to see him again was stronger than her relief; he would visit again, she felt sure.

While she was busy with the toddler Sister Cummins came into the room. 'Well, everything is fine,' she said in a satisfied voice. 'Mr Werdmer ter Sane is more than pleased—thinks everything is as near perfect as it can be. Mr Cresswell came with him, of course, he'll be in tomorrow morning again. Mr Werdmer ter Sane is going back to Holland this evening so I don't suppose we'll see him again. A pity. Now he wants the treatment changed—it's written up ...' She glanced at Rose. 'It's a good thing it's your weekend—you look washed out, Rose. Did the office allow you that week you wanted off?'

'Yes, thank you, Sister. That's in two weeks' time; I'm looking forward to it.'

'I won't say you're a lucky girl because you so deserve it, Rose. Now, as to this treatment, let's get it clear.'

There was plenty of work which was a good thing; she was too tired to think or mope when she went off duty, the days went quickly and the thought of her weekend off kept her going.

Aunt Millicent was glad to see her. Not a lady to show her feelings, nevertheless she had welcomed Rose with real warmth, and as for Maggie, that dear soul fussed round her like a hen with a chick; it was soothing to be made much of and under their kindness Rose's good sense began to take over from her black mood. It happens all the time, she told herself, girls falling in love with the wrong man, I just have to forget him and make up my mind to a career. Indeed, she actually told her aunt that she intended to apply for the post of junior night sister. 'Which will give me a chance to get a ward sister's post if one falls vacant,' she pointed out. 'It's a good jumping-off job.'

'Yes, if you wish to jump,' pointed out Aunt Millicent drily.

She wasn't a lady to invite or offer confidences but

she was well aware that Rose was unhappy and when it came to talking about her visit to Holland extremely cagey. 'It'll be that surgeon with the awkward name,' she informed Maggie as the pair of them watched Rose picking peas in the garden. 'And Rose being the girl she is, she'll break her heart silently.'

Old Maggie sighed. 'The dear soul, such a darling girl too! A wife in a million she'd be.' She sniffed. 'I'll make a Dundee cake for her to take back with her.'

They stood watching her, each of them loving her in their own way. Rose didn't tell her aunt about her visit to Holland until a short while before she had to go back to St Bride's. 'I like Christina very much,' she explained. 'It will be nice to see little Duert again.'

'And I dare say you'll meet some interesting people—friends of the ter Brandts,' observed Aunt Millicent casually.

'Oh, perhaps, they have a lovely house, I'll be quite happy just sitting around in the garden all day.'

'You'll go and see the girls you met at the hospital while you were there?' Her aunt's voice sounded uninterested.

'Perhaps. It's been a lovely weekend, Aunt Millicent, thank you.'

'Oh, pooh,' said her aunt gruffly, 'Maggie and I love to have you. Come again soon, my dear.'

CHAPTER SIX

THE summer weather had broken as Rose got off the bus and hurried through the rain to the hospital entrance. Slow drops of rain were falling and great clouds were piling up above her head. There would be a storm before morning and if the weather turned bad it would mean an evening in the sitting-room, drinking endless cups of tea and bandying hospital gossip. She took her case to her room and went down to the canteen for her supper and found most of her friends there. They greeted her noisily, all agog to tell her the news that Sadie had given in her notice. Alice, who always got hold of gossip before anyone else, said, 'She decided to get married just like that. Giving up nursing too, her Tom's been offered promotion and they've a chance of a house.' Alice added importantly, 'We're having a whip round to get her a present.'

Having delivered herself of this important piece of news she started on Rose. 'We never heard much about your job in Holland. Have you heard how the little boy is getting on? Your Shirley's doing awfully well. He's a wizard, isn't he, that Dutch surgeon? What's he like to work for?'

'Just as nice as Mr Cresswell,' said Rose, not wanting to talk about him. 'What are we going to get Sadie?'

There was plenty to do on the ward; little Shirley was well on the way to recovery and didn't need as much attention but there were several ill children and a battered baby, a poor scrap, undernourished, unloved and covered in bruises. With care he would become a normal baby again but it was going to take time and patience. Rose was glad to have something to keep her busy and her mind off her own affairs. And after a week, when the baby was beginning to look like a baby once more, she turned her mind to her holiday, only a week away now. Another dress, she decided, something she could wear in the evenings. She found a printed lawn with a frilled shawl collar and short full sleeves in a pale cyclamen pink, belted round her slim waist. She brought two or three T-shirts as well, in pastel colours, and a widely pleated deep cream skirt and cardigan to go with it. Trying them all on after duty she felt quite excited; it was unlikely that she would see Sybren Werdmer ter Sane, but if she did she wouldn't look too bad. Even Alice, that dampener of good spirits, observed that the dress did something for her.

She had heard from Christina; would she get herself a ticket on a morning flight to Amsterdam and someone would meet her there. There was a plane getting in at eleven o'clock, she had written, if Rose could get a seat on it, and if she couldn't would she let her know at once? So everything was arranged and Rose went on duty on a morning four days before she was due to start her holiday to find Mr Cresswell with Shirley.

'Just passing through,' he told Rose. 'I'll be back for a round; there's no need to get Sister Cummins.' He wandered to the door. 'I hear you're going over to Schiphol on Saturday, Rose, which flight?'

She was surprised but told him readily enough, and then gaped at him open-mouthed when he observed, 'My wife and I are travelling on that flight too. We'll see you on the plane if not before.'

'Oh—you're going on holiday, sir? I'm just going for a week to stay with Dr and Mevrouw ter Brandt.'

'Yes, yes, I know.' He wandered off through the door leaving her to wonder how he knew that, certainly she hadn't told him, still news had a way of getting round the hospital and she supposed that even as important a man as Mr Cresswell might stoop to listen to the grapevine occasionally.

Sadie was to take over from her for the week; now that she was going to leave she was spending her last month filling in for holidays and nurses off sick. Rose primed her well, promised to bring her back a box of the elaborate chocolates they had admired together when they had been on holiday, and packed her case. The weather hadn't broken, her week bid fair to be perfection. She washed her hair, bought a new lipstick and spent a long time applying varnish to her nails. She had pretty hands and she took care of them; the pearly pink varnish suited them very well.

She was at Heathrow in good time, unhurriedly getting herself through the routine. She was wearing one of the new T-shirts and the cream skirt and had tied back her hair with a matching ribbon and looked cool and uncluttered.

She hadn't expected to see Mr Cresswell and his wife, at least not until they were all on the plane, but as she went into the lounge, waiting to go on board, Mr Cresswell waved to her. 'Over here, Rose,' he commanded.

She went rather reluctantly; they got on well on the ward but now he was on holiday and his wife was with him. She had met Mrs Cresswell in the hospital, being taken round the wards to see the Christmas decorations, and she had liked her; a quiet unassuming woman, the antithesis of her husband's rather forceful manner. She smiled at Rose now and beckoned her to a seat beside her. 'So you're going to Holland too,' she stated comfortably. 'How long are you staying?'

'Only a week, with Dr ter Brandt and his family.'

Mrs Cresswell nodded. 'We're going for a fortnight but we're not staying in one place for more than a day or two. Do you like flying? I don't.'

They chatted in a desultory fashion until Mr Cresswell got to his feet as they were asked to board the plane, and Rose bade them goodbye, guessing that they were travelling first class, which they were.

She didn't see them at Schiphol; she had collected her case from the carousel and was making her way to a quiet corner to await whoever was to meet her when she found the Cresswells at her elbow.

'There you are,' declared Mr Cresswell, 'thought we'd missed you. And here's Sybren . . .'

And indeed it was, looking vast and very much at ease, kissing Mrs Cresswell, shaking Mr Cresswell by the hand and then as Rose took a step backwards, anxious to get away as fast as she could, flinging a casual arm round her shoulders which effectively rooted her to the spot. 'Hullo Rose,' he barely glanced at her. 'I'm dropping you off at the ter Brandts' place.' He picked up her case and led the way to where the car was parked, ushered Mrs Cresswell and Rose into the back, settled himself beside Mr Cresswell, and drove off.

Rose hadn't said a word. She had been surprised, filled with delight and now, having recovered her wits, indignant. It was like being a parcel, for indeed she had had no more chance to speak up for herself than a parcel would have. She said with only the faintest tremor of rage in her voice, 'I was expecting to be met . . .'

Mrs Cresswell patted her hand. 'Well, dear, I expect the ter Brandts thought this would be just as quick— Sybren dropping you off, I mean.'

It didn't seem worthwhile pointing out to her companion that he was going miles out of his way to do that; Schiphol was right on Amsterdam's doorstep, The Hague was well to the south. She smiled at Mrs Cresswell and fell to contemplating the back of Sybren's handsome head.

To her surprise they all got out when they reached the ter Brandts' house and from the lack of surprise on Corvinus's face, she concluded that they had been expected, all four of them.

Christina came into the hall then. 'Rose, isn't this fun?' She tucked an arm in hers as she greeted the Cresswells and lifted her face for Sybren's light kiss. 'Duert is on his way home, he'll be here in a few minutes. Sybren, take Mr Cresswell into the sitting-room and give him a drink while I take the girls upstairs.'

She led the way to a bedroom at the side of the house. 'Corvinus will bring your case up presently, Rose.' She beamed at her. 'I like your hair like that. There are combs and things on the dressing-table if you want anything.' She turned to Mrs Cresswell. 'How long are you staying with Sybren?'

'Just for two days, my dear. John wants to go to Leyden and then we're going to Friesland to join friends who are sailing there.'

They went unhurriedly downstairs and found Duert had joined his guests, and in the consequent flurry of greetings and handing of drinks, Rose found herself beside Mr Werdmer ter Sane. Light conversation was needed; she sought desperately for something to say, took a gulp of her sherry and did her best. 'What a lovely summer we're having,' she essayed.

'Weatherwise yes, otherwise no.' And when she looked at him, he gave her a bland smile which didn't help at all. But she persevered, 'Well, you have had one or two difficult cases, I expect.'

'Indeed I have.'

She said with desperate chattiness, 'Are you on holiday too?'

'No.' He looked at her. 'I like your hair like that.' He sighed gently. 'I always thought of you as rather a plain girl, but I see that I was wrong.'

It wasn't a conversation at all, thought Rose desperately, and everyone else was at the other end of the room. She took another good sip of sherry.

'No, you're not wrong, I'm plain; if you see something often enough you don't see it any more, if you see what I mean.'

'A muddled remark, but I get the gist. It is a pity that we can't be friends, Rose.'

She was finding the sherry a great help. 'Yes, it is, but it doesn't matter really, does it? We don't—we aren't—that is, we don't share the same backgroud, do we?' She added quite fiercely, 'I'm applying for a night sister's post when I get back.'

'Ah—a career girl.' He gave her a mocking smile and she felt a little sick because she would never be able to say the things she wanted to say to him, only pretend to an enthusiasm for something she had no heart for.

She was saved from answering by Christina who came over to join them and talk about the children. 'We're going to Noerdwijk-aan-zee,' she told them, 'for a picnic. You must come, Sybren, we are taking the children too, in a couple of days' time, and don't tell me you're operating because I know you're not.'

'My dear Chrissy, it sounds delightful, of course I'll come.' The others had joined them and presently they went in to lunch. And shortly after that he stowed his guests back into the car and drove away without having anything more to say to Rose.

Lying in her bed in her charming room after a blissful day, Rose allowed her thoughts to stray to Sybren. She hadn't expected him to be there although she admitted now that she had hoped that in some miraculous way they would meet again. But the meeting hadn't been very satisfactory; he had called her plain—well, not in so many words, but that was what he had meant. And she hadn't done anything about it; if she'd had any spirit at all she would have made him eat his words. There were ways ... she could have her hair permed and tinted and assemble a collection of lotions and creams and bright lipsticks. And new clothes, tight jeans and those enormous sweaters and layers of gossamer skirts and tops she had never been able to fathom in *Vogue*. He might look at her then and decide that she wasn't so plain after all.

She got out of bed and went over to the dressing-table and by the light of a brilliant moon bunched her long fine hair around her face, looping it up with one hand and turning and twisting to see the effect. Even by moonlight she could see that it wasn't for her.

She got back into bed, thinking now about her pleasant day; little Duert had remembered her and the baby was gorgeous. She and Christina had spent a lazy afternoon on the lawn behind the house with the baby in a Moses basket and the toddler tumbling between them. They had had their tea there too and then Dr ter Brandt had come home and he and Christina had gone indoors to bath the children and to give them

supper and feed them under Nanny's eye. It had been
nice to see Nanny again, and even nicer to be staying
with such a happy family. Half asleep, she wondered if
Sybren and that Mies girl would be happy.

The next day slipped by in a gentle round of gossip,
playing with the children, and when Dr ter Brandt
came home, an hour's run into the surrounding
country once the children were in bed. The roads he
took were well away from the motorways, narrow and
mostly brick-built, running between flat green mead-
ows, passing through small villages, very quiet
because as he explained it was the time of the evening
meal for most Dutch households. They went back
presently for drinks and dinner and afterwards friends
came in and spent an hour casually in the rather grand
drawing-room, rendered homely by Christina's
knitting cast down on a chair, the pile of papers lying
by the doctor's big wing chair and the two dogs,
wandering from one to the other. A lovely day,
thought Rose, lying in her bed already half asleep, and
an even lovelier tomorrow because they were going on
a picnic and Sybren would be there.

He arrived about ten o'clock in time to have coffee
before they set out. They went in Dr ter Brandt's
Rolls with the girls in the back with the children and
Sybren in front, the impedimenta necessary for a day's
picnicking bestowed in the boot. 'So small,' observed
the baby's doting father, 'and half the contents of the
house seem necessary for her comfort.'

He exchanged a smile with Christina and Rose
thought wistfully how marvellous it must be to be
married to someone who loved you and you loved too.
She looked away and found Mr Werdmer ter Sane's
eyes fixed so intently upon her that she put a hand up
to her hair; she hadn't even bothered to tie it back but

left it to hang down her back. He smiled suddenly and she smiled rather shyly back at him; perhaps it was because he was wearing slacks and an open-necked shirt that he seemed friendly.

Noerdwijk-aan-zee was small, tucked among the dunes, with a single main street, a line of hotels along the short boulevard and a wide beach stretching as far as the eye could see in either direction and although there were plenty of people on the sands there was room and to spare; besides, the ter Brandts had a beach hut at the quieter end where the small town ended and the dunes took over. The hut opened, rugs and cushions and a sun umbrella arranged, the picnic basket and the children's needs dealt with, Christina declared that she was going for a swim before they had lunch. She gave her husband a speaking glance as she said this and he said at once, 'A splendid idea, darling, we can leave these two to baby-sit and they can have a turn while we put the food and drink ready.'

The baby was asleep and little Duert busy with a bucket and spade. Rose sat with her back against the hut wall, watching him, while Sybren lay full length on his back, his eyes closed.

But he wasn't asleep. Still with his eyes closed he remarked, 'There is a great deal to be said for the domestic life, don't you agree, Rose?'

She looked towards the sea where the ter Brandts were swimming side by side. 'Oh yes.' She spoke in a rather colourless voice, afraid that she might betray her feelings, longing to be in Christina's shoes, only of course Sybren would be in Dr ter Brandt's and little Duert would be another Sybren and the baby . . . what would they call the baby?

'Stop dreaming, Rose. Tell me, do you suppose I should make a good husband?'

She said carefully, 'I imagine that any man would make a good husband if he loved his wife.'

'Don't beg the question.'

'You see, I've worked for you in hospital and seen you there but I don't know anything about you. You have a lovely home and I dare say lots of friends. I think you work very hard and like your work and you're successful, aren't you? You're handsome too.' She spoke matter-of-factly, while her heart cried out at the idea of him being anyone's husband but hers. 'That evening at the restaurant in The Hague, there was a lovely girl with you—I don't know her name; Christina called her Mies. Are you going to marry her?'

He opened one eye. 'You think that she would make me a suitable wife?'

She said severely, 'How could I possibly tell, Mr Werdmer ter Sane?'

'My name Sybren. Do I seem very middle-aged to you, Rose?'

She shot upright with real surprise. 'Middle-aged, you're joking. Why, you're—you're not even in the prime of your life.'

He rolled over and sat up. 'Well, that's something. It encourages me to make a sandcastle with my godson.'

Which he proceeded to do. The pair of them were still busy with it when the ter Brandts came strolling back from their swim.

'The water is just right,' Christina flung herself down beside Rose.

'Whip into your swimsuit. Rose, Duert and I will get the lunch.' She looked across at Sybren. 'Are you going in, Sybren?'

He glanced up from the careful tunnel he was making. 'Yes, what about this young man?'

'He's going swimming with his Papa, aren't you, my dear?' She cast a motherly eye at the Moses basket. 'Off with you while I lay the cloth.'

Sybren seemed in no hurry; Rose went away to change into her swim suit, a sensible affair in navy blue, plaited her hair and wound it into a topknot and went off down the beach to where the doctor and his small son were paddling. The water was pleasantly warm and very clear. She waded slowly and then began to swim, something she could do well. After a little while she paused to tread water and rest and saw Sybren beside her.

'You swim well.'

'Thank you. I used to swim with my father; I'm rather out of practice.'

He had turned on to his back and she did the same. It was blissfully warm and quiet and she could have stayed there for ever; somehow everything seemed so simple, just the two of them floating around in a kind of limbo. What would he say if she told him she loved him? A kind of recklessness seized her and she actually had her mouth open to ask him when he turned over and began to swim slowly towards the shore. 'Time for lunch,' he told her.

She reached the beach at the same time as he, trembling with a kind of delayed shock at what she might have said. He gave her a sharp glance as they waded ashore. 'Cold?' he wanted to know. 'You are shivering.' He added kindly, 'You'd better get some clothes on.'

She felt better by the time she had dressed and joined the others, and over their leisurely meal she became her usual composed self again, keeping an eye on little Duert, sampling the wafer-thin sandwiches and little cheese tartlets, the salad, the hard boiled eggs, the ham *broodjes*, and drinking the lager, icy cold from its container. There was hot coffee afterwards, too, and while she and Christina settled the little ones for a nap the men packed everything away and then strolled off along the sands.

'It's nice here, isn't it?' said Christina. 'It's our favourite picnic place.' She smiled dreamily. 'We—we got engaged here.'

Rose rolled over to look at her. 'Oh, did you? How romantic, was it a lovely day like today?'

Christina chuckled. 'There was a gale blowing and it rained torrents. But that didn't matter.'

Rose sighed without knowing it. 'No, I don't suppose it would.' She looked along the beach to where in the distance the two men were strolling along. 'When I get back I'm going to apply for a night sister's post—the junior one.'

'You like night-duty?'

She shook her head. 'No, but it's the quickest way to get promotion, isn't it?'

'You want to stay at St Bride's?' Christina sounded casual.

'Well, I expect I'd better; perhaps when I've had a senior post for a year or two, I'll try for somewhere else.'

'Do you mind where?'

She shook her head again. 'No—it doesn't matter.'

'Don't you want to get married?'

She sat up, glancing without meaning to at the two men, coming towards them now. 'Yes, oh, yes. But I shan't so I'll have to be a career girl.'

The two men joined them and they sat around, not talking much, until the children woke and they fetched cold drinks from the picnic basket and then packed

everything up, climbed into the car and drove back to
The Hague.

Nanny was waiting to see to little Duert and the
baby and Rose went to her room and showered and
put on a fresh dress and went back downstairs to find
the others already on the patio and Corvinus arranging
the tea tray just so. She would have liked the next hour
to last for ever; sitting in the late afternoon sunshine,
listening to the gentle talk around her but not having
much to say for herself. They had been discussing a
play at the Koninklijke Schouwburg and idly
wondering if they should go one evening when Sybren
observed, 'Which reminds me I must be going—I've a
date this evening.' He looked hard at Rose. 'Dinner
with Mies.'

She looked straight back at him. 'All this fresh air
will have given you a splendid appetite.' She said it
just a bit too quickly and at his sudden smile, looked
away.

'A delightful day,' he remarked as he got up. 'We
must do it again some time. Kiss the babies good night
for me, Christina.' He bent and kissed her cheek, said
something in Dutch to Deurt ter Brandt and turned to
Rose. 'I'll see you again, Rose,' and watched the
delight flood her face before she could prevent it. He
bent suddenly and pulled her to her feet. 'See me to
the car, the exercise will do you good.'

The car was at the front of the house; she walked
beside him in silence along the patio and round the
corner to the sweep before the door where the Rolls
stood. When they reached it she said sedately, 'I hope
you have a lovely evening.'

He stood looking down at her, half smiling. She
supposed it was a silly remark to make and not worth
an answer. He said softly, 'I'm working all day

tomorrow, the day after that I'm coming to fetch you before lunch—you can tell Christina I'll bring you back safely after dinner in the evening.'

'But you haven't asked me—I haven't said I'll come . . .' Her voice shook a little with happy excitement and she hoped it sounded as it usually did.

For answer he caught her close and kissed her. She hadn't been kissed very often and never like this. He let her go very gently, got into the car and drove away, leaving her standing with her mouth open and her eyes wide.

She stayed where she was for a few moments while a succession of thoughts wove their way through her head. Almost all of them made nonsense; a number of them were the stuff of which dreams are made; only a very few were sensible. With a great effort she allowed these to take over; Sybren was no boy; he had had years in which to bring kissing to a fine art; doubtless he kissed all the girls with equal finesse. He was probably feeling sentimental at the prospect of seeing Mies and last but not least he might have kissed her in a fit of absent-mindedness. The last was hard to swallow but it was as good a reason as any. She walked slowly back to where the ter Brandts were sitting to be greeted by Christina's cheerful, 'Seen him off in that car of his? A pity he couldn't stay to dinner.'

Rose stooped to pat the dogs. 'Yes, he's asked me to go out with him the day after tomorrow—for lunch, he said he'd bring me back in the evening after dinner, if that is all right with you.'

She didn't see Christina's wide grin at her husband. 'Oh, lovely for you—we hadn't planned anything, had we, Duert? You'll be able to see some more of Amsterdam. We wondered if you'd like to go to Scheveningen tomorrow? It's a bit crowded but there's the pier and lots to see. Duert's given himself a day off again; at least what he calls a day off—he'll go to the hospital early and be home by ten o'clock or so and then go in again beetween tea and dinner. The weather forecast's good, we'll take the children and the dogs for a walk before we go and leave them with Nanny.'

It sounded fun, thought Rose, besides she would be able to take her mind off Sybren.

It was as much fun as she had hoped even though the wretched man wasn't out of her head for one single second. They had put the baby in her pram, attached little Duert to his leading reins and with the dogs for escort taken a walk through the quiet avenues around the house and by the time they had got back Duert was waiting for them. There was no hurry; they sat for a while playing with the children and gossiping before they got into the car. That was the nice part about living as the ter Brandts did; no one seemed fussed about time or being late or having to get somewhere; she supposed it was because they had a beautifully run home and devoted staff. She had a sudden memory of racing on and off duty at St Bride's always with an eye on the clock, calculating how much one could get done in a given time on the ward, or just how long it would take to get to the station or go shopping. She sank back, relishing the comfort of the car and sternly stopped her thoughts from wandering to Sybren. He would be working himself now, doing a round or perhaps operating. She jumped guiltily as Duert said over his shoulder, 'I saw Sybren—he was at my hospital to see a child with brain damage. I'm to remind you that he'll be with us by eleven o'clock tomorrow.'

Rose murmured something and wished she didn't blush so easily.

They went first to the harbour so that she could see the fishing boats and the fishermen's wives in their voluminous black skirts and coloured shawls, their heads covered in snowy caps with the gold ornaments on either side. And having had her fill of these, they drove back along the long promenade to the casino where Duert parked the car while they went on to the pier. It was delightful loitering in the sun, sitting down to drink lemonade and watch the crowds on the beach.

'Is it always as crowded as this?' asked Rose.

'No, only in July and August. We hardly ever come; sometimes in the autumn, it's so quiet then; no one about, only the fishermen.'

They lunched at Le Bon Ton, a French bistro, small but Rose guessed that it was expensive. Afterwards they got into the car again and went to Madurodam, the miniature model city halfway between Scheveningen and The Hague. Here they spent more than an hour, treading between the miniature houses and shops, watching the trains and trams travelling to and fro and they saw the barges on the canals sailing slowly along, while the windmills turned, ferries fussed back and forth and in the harbour boats came and went and the planes landed and took off from the airfield.

'Pretty marvellous, isn't it?' observed Duert. 'It lights up in the evening you know.'

'Why is it called Madurodam? Is there a town called that in Holland?'

'No, it's named after a lieutenant, George Maduro, who died in Dachau. There couldn't be a better memorial, could there?'

They went back to the beach then, and walked along the firm sand by the water's edge and returned finally

to have tea in the pier restaurant. 'A lovely day,' said
Rose and meant it, finding it even lovelier because in
the morning she would see Sybren again.

He was very punctual but all the same she had been
ready for half an hour before he arrived. She was
wearing the pink dress and had taken extra care with
her face and hair. She had put it up at first, and then
taken all the pins out and brushed it smooth and tied it
back with a pink ribbon. Soon enough she would be
wearing it in a severe bun again, she reminded herself.
Only one more day left after this day and then back to
St Bride's and hard work. She couldn't bear to think
of it.

She had felt a little shy at meeting Sybren again but
she didn't need to; he greeted her with casual
friendliness, observed that he was glad to see that she
wasn't going to keep him waiting, spent five minutes
talking to Christina and the children, then stowed her
in the car, got in beside her and drove off.

She didn't ask where they were going, she was
content enough just to sit there beside him. When they
reached his house she got out to find Hans waiting by
the open door, his face wreathed in smiles. She wished
him good day and added, 'Do you remember me,
Hans?'

'Certainly, Miss, a pleasure to see you again.'

The hall was cool and dim and this time she was
ushered into a room on the other side of it, smaller
than the rather grand one she remembered from her
first visit. But it was beautiful, nonetheless, with
panelled walls hung with paintings, comfortable chairs
and little tables scattered around and a deep window
at one end with a window seat piled with cushions.
Curled up among them was a black and white cat who
took no notice of them at all, nor twitched a whisker

when the door behind them was thrust wide and a
bouvier came prancing in. Rose had glimpsed one
once or twice on her previous visits to Holland but she
had never been as close as this. He looked a bit
fearsome with his small yellow eyes and great head but
she put out a clenched fist for his inspection and bade
him a polite hello.

He went to his master first, wagging his stumpy tail
and beaming all over his ferocious face and then at a
word from Sybren gently nosed Rose's hand and
offered his head for a pat.

'William,' said Sybren, 'and don't ask me why. I've
had him since he was a very small puppy and he'll not
harm a hair of your head.' He turned to look at her.
'He knows you belong here, you see.'

She had nothing to say to that; he went on, 'He
would make mincemeat of anyone I didn't approve of,
though. You like him?'

'Oh, yes, very much. What does he do all day while
you're at the hospital?'

'We go for a walk each morning before breakfast
and again in the evening. I'm not always away from
home, you know. When I'm free we go to the woods
or to the beach and he loves riding in the car. During
the day Hans takes him out.'

He strolled over to a sofa table behind a brocade
sofa. 'What will you drink, Rose?'

And when she hesitated: 'Will you try a long drink?
Sherry and tonic with ice? Just right for this weather.'

She found that she wasn't shy with him any more;
they had slipped into an easy relationship which
permitted of companionable silence as well as talk and
presently they crossed the hall again to the dining-
room, at the back of the house, a panelled room and
furnished very beautifully with a mahogany oval table

and chairs and a serving table against one wall. There was a magnificent *stoelklok* on one wall and a vast mirror in a carved frame over the wide hearth. They sat at one end of the table and ate without haste, pausing to talk a great deal. There were potted shrimps, lamb cutlets with potato straws and mouthwatering salad and by way of afters orange ice cream with Courvoisier, all these helped along very nicely with a muscadet and rounded off with coffee served in paper-thin china cups and poured from a massive silver coffee-pot.

Rose accepted it all, as she would accept a lovely dream, querying nothing, knowing at the same time that dreams have a way of ending and that she would wake up presently. But she refused to think of that, just for a little while she was truly happy.

After lunch he took her round the house, so much bigger than it appeared from the street with a vast complex of kitchens and pantries and cellars below ground where she met Hans' wife Jultsje, a big woman with bright blue eyes and a wide smile, and a round dumpling of a girl who grinned and blushed. Hanna was from Friesland just as Jultsje was, being that lady's niece. 'There is also a gardener, but he's quite old and comes and goes when he likes,' explained Sybren leading the way up the narrow staircase which opened into the back of the hall.

Upstairs there were any number of rooms, some large and beautifully furnished with modern bathrooms cunningly hidden away and some small and cosy, tucked away down narrow passages or up short narrow stairs. It took some time to see everything and when they got back to the big room she remembered so well, the afternoon was almost over.

'We'll have a stroll in the garden, shall we?' asked

Sybren and took her out to the long narrow lawn behind the house with William at his heels. They strolled round the garden afterwards and half way down its well ordered length he stopped to say, 'I like your dress, Rose. You should always wear pink.' He bent and kissed her cheek lightly and then walked on again, his hand under her arm. 'After dinner we'll go for a stroll along the *grachten*.' And after that he talked about commonplace things; Amsterdam and his home and how the city had changed over the last few years and the differences between Dutch and English law, and Rose sitting beside him on a little rustic seat built round the mulberry tree at the very end of the garden listened to every word.

They went back into the house presently, into the vast drawing-room where Hans had set tea on a drum-table by the window. Rose was pouring their tea when Sybren came and took his cup from her and set it on the table.

He said quite angrily, 'Dammit, there's something I want to say to you—something—I must explain before you go back to England. The trouble with you is that I thought that I knew what you were thinking; now I've got to know you better I'm not sure any more. I'm not even sure if you like me.'

She looked at him then and smiled a little and said steadily, 'Oh, yes, I like you, I didn't mean to though.'

'Good. Rose, what would you say if I were to tell you that I want to get married?' He paused. 'Do you know me well enough, I wonder?'

He was standing in front of her, for once in his self-assured life at a loss for words, staring down at her plain face so very composed. Her composure was like a fence between them although he had no idea that he had only to give it the slightest push to get rid of it. He began, 'Rose . . .'

She held her breath, not sure what was going to happen next, aware that her insides were turning over and over wondering what he was going to say.

Only he didn't say it; the telephone rang.

CHAPTER SEVEN

MR WERDMER TER SANE said something in his own language. He spoke softly and Rose couldn't understand him, which was just as well because he was swearing quite ferociously. He went to the phone and listened without comment and she watched his face change back to the blandness she didn't much care for. When he spoke it was to utter only a few words before he put the phone down. He looked at her across the room and she wondered how a face could change so swiftly from warmth to an impersonal politeness; just as though she had arrived unexpectedly and he had felt he had to ask her to stay to tea . . .

'Don't go—have your tea; I shouldn't be long . . . I'll let you know.'

Something at the hospital, she supposed, something serious too, otherwise why should he have changed from the delightful companion who had shared her day to this polite distant man. She said quietly: 'Very well, Sybren,' and watched him go from the room. He put his head round the door a moment later.

'It's only fair to tell you that that was Mies.'

She felt as though she had been turned to stone. What was fair about it? And what was she supposed to make of his remark? And why in heaven's name had he made it? She sat there while the tea cooled in her cup. Hans came in presently, took a look at the untouched sandwiches and cakes and took away the teapot and the teacups and came back with fresh tea.

'Mijnheer wouldn't like it if you do not eat and

drink, Miss,' he cautioned her. So she drank some tea
and ate a couple of sandwiches and watched the
beautiful little carriage clock on the mantelpiece.
Almost an hour went by before the phone rang again,
and this time Hans was in the room to answer it
before she could get out of her chair. 'For you,
Miss,' he told her and went softly from the room.

'That is Rose Comely?' asked a voice; a high little
tinkling voice, and Rose knew who it was at once. She
said, 'Yes, you wanted me?'

'I have a message. Sybren will not be back at his
house. He sends his regrets and you are to ask Hans to
see you back to The Hague.'

'Why is he not coming back here?' asked Rose.

Mies laughed. 'That is something you will know, but
not just this evening. We celebrate—you understand?'

Rose had no chance to ask any more questions; Mies
rang off.

She went and sat down for a few minutes, trying to
understand. Why couldn't Sybren have spoken to her
himself? And was that what he had been on the point
of telling her when Mies had phoned him? There was
no point in guessing, she thought wearily, and went in
search of Hans, who listened politely to her rather
muddled request, assured her that he would get out
the second car from the garage and drive her back
himself. 'For that is what Mijnheer would wish,' he
told her. 'You will not stay for dinner, Miss?'

To dine alone in the splendour of Sybren's dining-
room would have been farcical. She refused politely
and waited until he went to fetch the car. A Rover,
beautifully polished. She got in beside Hans and
maintained a conversation of sorts for the entire
journey although afterwards she had no idea what she
had said.

The ter Brandts were sitting together having drinks before dinner when she arrived. Hans, with a tact which she thanked him for from the bottom of her heart, had rung the bell and gone inside, presumably to explain, for a moment later Christina came out to the car, poked her head through the window and said cheerfully. 'Called out, was he? It happens all the time, Rose. You're just in time for a drink before dinner.'

She was swept into the house, and Hans, suitably thanked, went off to the kitchen for coffee before going back to Amsterdam. 'You'll tell Mister Werdmer ter Sane that I quite understood, won't you?' Rose begged him. 'You won't forget.'

She had her drink and ate her dinner, looking, if she had but known, as though the world had come to an end, as indeed it had for her. But neither Christina or Duert said anything, but embarked on a lengthy discussion as to whether they should spend Christmas in London or at home, which meant that she could sit between them and murmur from time to time without actually taking part in the conversation. Presently Christina said easily: 'You must be dog tired, Rose. Don't stand on ceremony with us, if you'd like an early night.'

So she went to bed, but not to sleep; she thought about Sybren until her head ached. But not as much as her heart.

Mr Werdmer ter Sane wasn't thinking about her; he was bent over the operating table very carefully removing a blood clot from the brain of a small boy who had fallen out of a fifth-floor window from a block of flats in one of the poorer parts of Amsterdam. That the child was alive was partly due to Mies van Toule who had been taking a short cut through the city in her car and had been forced to stop by a distraught woman who demanded that she should go to the nearest telephone and get help. Her inclination had been to drive on but then she remembered that her dearest friend had told her that Sybren had been seen driving that morning with a girl beside him. She had guessed, quite rightly, that it had been Rose, probably she was at his house now; she had noticed the difference in Sybren's manner of late and this was a chance to get even. She had phoned his house, knowing that he would go at once to the hospital and when he had seen her at the hospital and asked her to phone Rose and explain, she had played the perfect helpful friend and promised to do so. It had all worked out very nicely; she had driven a wedge very neatly between Sybren and Rose. And being clever as well as pretty, she drove herself out of Amsterdam to stay with friends without telling anyone where she was going, thus avoiding possible awkward questions from Sybren.

He wasn't free to phone his home until well after midnight and Hans told him then that he had driven Rose back to The Hague and then delivered her message. Mr Werdmer ter Sane had grunted some reply, told Hans to go to bed and then gone back to the intensive care unit; the child was by no means out of danger.

He got home at four o'clock in the morning; the child, despite all his efforts, had died. He drank the coffee in the flask left out for him by the faithful Hans, showered and changed his clothes and went to his study; sleep was out of the question, he found himself wishing that Rose was there, sitting quietly listening while he went over his night. Sitting there too tired to sleep, he knew that she was all that he wanted. Which was strange, he mused, smiling to himself, he had had no inkling that he would grow to love her when they had first met. Later, when he had finished his morning round at the hospital he would go to The Hague and tell her so. He yawned hugely and closed his eyes and Hans found him there a few hours later, sitting in his great chair asleep.

He was delayed at the hospital. Too late to go to his home for lunch, he ate a sandwich and drank his coffee at the hospital and then got into his car. He was tired now but to see Rose was more important than sleep.

Rose had packed that morning and now she was on the lawn beyond the house with the baby asleep in her pram, little Duert curled up on a rug under the trees and Nanny dozing in a chair close by. Christina had gone to the hairdresser and Duert was at the hospital and they would all forgather for tea presently. She had cried her eyes out during the night and now there were no tears left. Tomorrow she would go back to England and Sybren must and would be forgotten. It wouldn't have been so bad, she thought for the hundredth time, if he had told her that he was going to marry Mies; after all she had guessed that for herself, but it had hurt, his bald message without explaining, and Mies . . . Rose ground her splendid teeth at the thought of the girl. She had heard the triumph in the girl's voice over the phone. Rose rolled over on to her front; well, good luck to them both.

She didn't hear Mr Werdmer ter Sane's silent approach, and since her three companions were by now all fast asleep, they didn't hear him either.

He had stretched himself out beside her while she was still catching her breath. He said quietly, 'I'm sorry our day had to end like that, Rose.'

She said stonily, 'Please don't apologise. Mies explained. Although I can't think why you couldn't have done that for yourself.' Her voice had risen slightly despite her best efforts to keep it nonchalant.

'I was unable to phone you myself.' She glanced at him and he at her. 'I didn't get home until morning.'

Rose sat up straight, her imagination running wild. 'I don't suppose you did.' She gave a snort. 'Celebrating . . . I cannot for the life of me think why you asked me out yesterday; it was quite unnecessary, you know. I couldn't care less if I never see you again, not that I shall so that won't matter.' She gave a great heaving breath, got to her feet and raced away into the house and up to her room, where she walked up and down pausing to look out of the window at Sybren, lying where she had left him on the grass. He looked as though he was asleep and in fact he was.

Of course she had to go down again when Christina came home. She had pulled herself together very nicely and she need not have worried about Sybren; his manner towards her was pleasantly casual, just sufficiently interested in her return to England but evincing no curiosity as to what she intended doing when she got there. Only once, when she happened to catch his eyes inadvertently, did she see the anger in it.

I'm the one to be angry, she thought, listening with a serene face to Christina's plans for Christmas. Christmas seemed a long way off; and where would she be? Rose wondered. On night-duty, more than likely.

Mr Werdmer ter Sane got up to leave. He had refused an invitation to stay to dinner, pleading a previous engagement, but without drawing attention to herself, there was no way in which Rose could refuse his request to accompany him to his car.

She walked beside him, giving the strong impression that she was ready to turn tail and run at any moment and he had nothing to say until they reached the car.

'Where did you think I went yesterday evening?' he wanted to know in a casual voice.

Rose had herself nicely in hand. 'You told me—at least you told me that Mies had telephoned . . . You said it was only fair to tell me.'

He sounded amused. 'And am I to be allowed to explain or are you to stay like a poker?'

'You have no need to explain and it isn't funny . . . Mies explained, just as you told her to.'

He had stopped by the car and now he lent against it, his hands in his pockets, looking so casual she had a strong wish to box his ears if that were physically possible. 'And she said?' he prompted blandly.

'That you—both of you—were together—she said I'd understand . . .'

'And you understood, of course?' His voice was soft.

'I'm not a fool,' said Rose fiercely. Before she could say more, he asked. 'And of course you believed her?'

'Why not?' she snapped. 'I may be plain and uninteresting but I won't be pitied—or patronised. You had no right to invite me to spend the day with you and let me think . . .' She stopped before she gave herself away. 'I suppose you thought you were giving me a treat.'

'You thought that of me, Rose?' His voice was harsh.

She didn't know what she thought any more. 'I never want to see you or speak to you again,' she flung at him, 'and I hope you'll both be very happy.'

She turned and ran back to the house and after a moment Sybren got into his car and drove away.

The ter Brandts were sitting where she had left them. They looked at her stricken face and Duert said at once, 'We were just talking about your journey home. I've given myself a half-day and we'll all drive down to Schiphol and see you off. We'll be over ourselves before Christmas and we must see something of you then.'

Christina chimed in then, full of ideas and plans, talking easily, giving Rose time to become more the self-contained girl that she was. They left her presently while they went to see the children into bed and she sat on in the cool early evening, her miserable thoughts going round in her head like mice on a wheel. Presently she got up and went up to her room to tidy herself for the evening, wondering what she would do and say if Sybren were to phone. He didn't of course and when she went down to join the ter Brandts she astonished herself and them with her bright chattiness for the rest of the evening.

'Can't we do something?' begged Christina after she had said good night. 'I do wonder what happened . . .?'

'Well, my love, you will have to be patient,' said Duert, 'we can't possibly interfere.'

'No? Couldn't you possibly just hint . . .'

'No, darling. Sybren may be one of my closest friends, but I won't poke my nose into his affairs.'

'I bet that beastly Mies is at the bottom of it,' observed Christina.

Duert went to the hospital directly after breakfast with the promise that he would be back for an early lunch and Christina and Rose spent the morning in the garden, playing with the children and gossiping idly.

'Are you on duty tomorrow?' asked Christina.

'Yes—half past seven in the morning too. It feels as

though I've been away for several weeks instead of seven days. I've had such a gorgeous time.'

Rose's pale face belied the words but Christina didn't comment. 'We've loved having you and remember we're going to see something of you before the end of the year. Will you be night sister by then?'

'I'm not sure—I might not even get the post, but if I do I believe the job starts next month.' Thinking about it, she viewed the prospect with something like dismay.

The morning slid away with her ears stretched for a telephone call which never came and after lunch she was driven to Schiphol to be given a send-off she wouldn't forget, with an armful of flowers and chocolates and warm goodbyes which did something to melt the hard cold knot in her chest.

It was hot and thundery when she got on the bus at Heathrow and as she got out at the terminal great drops of rain began to fall so that once in London she gave way to the extravagence of a taxi to St Bride's. The sky was dark overhead by now and the hospital, never a thing of beauty, looked gloomy and uninviting and when she got to her room it was to find none of her friends off-duty, so she unpacked, got her uniform ready for the morning and went down to supper.

All her close friends were there; over egg and chips, bread-and-butter pudding and cups of tea she painted an enviable picture of her holiday.

'Lucky you,' declared Sadie, 'while we've all been slaving away . . . there's a new houseman, though!'

There was a ripple of laughter round the table. 'You'll never guess his name, Rose. Percy Pride, he's quite a lad too—this is his first job and he's very pleased with himself.' Sadie examined her nails. 'I've been out with him—just for supper.' She heaved a sigh. 'I must say I'll miss the odd date when I'm married.'

She shot a look at Rose. 'Did you have a date while you were in The Hague?'

Rose had already told them about the picnic and one could hardly call her fiasco of a day out with Sybren a date. 'No,' and she added lamely, 'there wasn't time—we were always doing something.'

They all liked her too much to pursue the matter and presently, since they were off-duty now, they went over to the home and spent their usual hour or so drinking more tea and eating the packet of Dutch biscuits Rose had had the forethought to bring with her.

She went back on duty to Sister Cummins' ward and found it busier than ever. Little Shirley was making progress, but slowly, and nursing her was a painstaking chore that had to be kept to with exact strictness. Mr Cresswell who was still away had restricted the operating list to routine stuff which his registrar dealt with in his absence.

On her first morning back, Rose met the new houseman. He seemed pleasant enough and anxious to be friendly and impress her, and Rose, being Rose, took him at face value and thought he wasn't too bad. He had a lot to say for himself but the young housemen often had; they were pleased that they had jobs and she didn't blame them for that. She had, in her own modest way, been pleased with herself when she had been awarded the gold medal. Not that she ever mentioned it to anyone.

A day or two slipped by, she wrote her thank-you letter to Christina, phoned Aunt Millicent and was warmly invited to spend her next free days with her, and over and above that she took care to spend her off-duty time with one or other of her friends: that way she didn't find it so easy to lapse into thoughts of Sybren. Only at bedtime did she allow herself to do that; he was the last thing she thought of before she slept and each morning when she woke her first thought was that perhaps by some miracle, he would turn up at St Bride's.

She would have to wait until the end of the following week before she could have her weekend but she was due a day off before then. It surprised her very much when Percy Pride followed her into the office one morning and asked her what she was going to do with it.

She was searching through the charts on the desk and answered rather carelessly, 'Oh, nothing much. Have a good sleep and do some window-shopping.'

Percy was looking at himself in Sister's looking glass. He was a conceited young man but his ego, flattened by Sadie's flippant treatment, needed a boost. And who better to do that than Rose, unremarkable and at a loose end? She would be grateful for his attentions and once he felt sure of himself again, he could pass on to some of the pretty nurses he had noticed around the place. He arranged himself negligently on the side of Sister's desk. 'How about having lunch with me? I'm free until the morning—we might try a picture gallery or a museum afterwards.'

Rose had the charts nicely arranged. 'Do get off the desk,' she begged him, 'I've just got things sorted . . . Thank you, I'd like to come out with you.' She sounded pleased and he puffed out his chest, not knowing that she would have accepted an invitation from just about anyone because that was the only way she could try to forget Sybren.

He got off the desk. 'Splendid. Twelve o'clock in the front hall?' He added rather grandly, 'I'll be back to check that nephritis. Let me know if you are worried.'

He walked off, pleased with himself, leaving Rose wondering what on earth had possessed her to accept his invitation. Still, it would get her through another day and each day would be easier, she told herself.

'He's not quite your type,' said Sadie when Rose told her.

'What's my type, then?'

'Oh, someone older, love. Someone who could see what you're really like.'

'You mean under my plain face there's a heart of gold?'

Sadie giggled. 'Something like that, but our Percy will do for you to practise on, only don't let him practise on you.' She got off the bed to pour more tea for them both. 'I say, I've been thinking, would it be a good idea if the bridesmaids wore pink but in different shades—light to dark if you see what I mean, and how do you feel about a wreath of flowers or do you want a hat?'

Percy Pride was quite forgotten in the serious business of Sadie's wedding.

They went back on duty together and Rose went straight on to the ward so that the part-time staff nurse could go to her dinner, leaving her with a first-year nurse and Mrs MacCauley, a sensible middle-aged nursing auxiliary. She was checking little Shirley's T.P.R. while the other two did the after-dinner tidying round when Mr Werdmer ter Sane walked on to the ward. Rose turned her head to see what the slight commotion was behind her and saw him coming unhurriedly towards her. She charted the board, which gave her a few seconds to steady herself, but nothing would stop the colour flooding to her face, nor could it check her racing heart. All the same her 'Good afternoon, Sir,' was uttered in a calm voice.

He stood and looked at her for a moment, smiling in that nasty way, she supposed because she was blushing so fiercely. His 'Good afternoon, Staff,' was uttered with a brisk politeness. 'I saw Mr Cresswell a day or so ago and told him that I would cast an eye over Shirley.'

'Yes, Sir, I'll get the registrar.'

'He knows I'm here.' He sat down on the side of the cot and began a conversation with Shirley. After a moment he looked over his shoulder at Rose. 'Are you free this evening?'

'No,' said Rose much too fast, and the blush which had almost gone, started all over again.

'Tomorrow?'

'I have a day off; I'm spending it with one of the housemen . . .'

He raised his eyebrows. 'Are you? Nice work, Rose. I take it I'm not forgiven?'

'No.' She didn't meet his eyes. 'Would you like to see the wound? It's healing well but there's just one area that's oozing . . .'

She looked up with relief as the registrar with Percy Pride at his heels joined them, and Mr Werdmer ter Sane fell to poking and prodding very gently. At length he straightened himself. 'Yes, well I think we're in the clear.' He looked at Rose. 'Is she chesty?'

'Yes—not much, but I noticed it for the first time this morning.'

'Nurse quite rightly reported it to me,' interrupted Percy Pride, and was interrupted in his turn by

Sybren's quite quiet: 'Nurse? which nurse? Or do you refer to Staff Nurse Comely?'

'Oh, er—yes. Sorry. I've written her up for a mist: expect:'

Mr Werdmer ter Sane looked at the registrar who looked back at him with a poker face, and Rose knowing exactly what was going to happen picked up the chart and handed it to him. 'We don't want a nasty chest, do we?' he enquired mildly. 'Ampycillin, I think—the linctus of course.' He glanced at Rose. 'Keep an eye open, Staff Nurse, and let me know if you're worried. I'm here for a few days.'

He handed her the chart back. 'Good day to you and thank you.'

The three of them went away and she nodded at the student nurse who hurried down the ward to open the door and came back beaming with pleasure because Sybren had paused to thank her as though he really meant it.

Rose saw him again the next day; she had gone to the entrance hall at noon precisely only to be told by Bagg the head porter that Mr Pride would be delayed for a few minutes. She was mooning round, examining the marble busts of bygone surgeons and physicians which littered the hall, when Mr Werdmer ter Sane came through the entrance door. Since she was facing the door at that moment she couldn't pretend that she hadn't seen him. He walked unhurriedly towards her, his eyebrows lifted.

He said, very suave, 'Staff Nurse Comely—about to enjoy your day off?' He looked around him in what she considered to be a sickeningly smug manner. 'Percy not turned up? I must say I consider that you could have done better for yourself.'

She was stung into saying most unwisely, 'Beggars

can't be choosers.' And regretted the words immediately because he said cheerfully, 'I did offer to bury the hatchet; we could have done so most amicably over lunch at Wilton's. Champagne of course; I always placate my enemies with champagne—mushrooms in cream sauce, lobster thermidor, and raspberries and cream . . .'

Rose who had eaten a slice of toast and had a mug of tea with a tea bag for her breakfast, said crossly, 'Oh, be quiet do,' and then, 'I'm not your enemy, I just don't like you.'

'Yes, you said so and that you weren't going to speak to me again.'

'Well, I have to on the ward and it—it would be rude if I pretended not to see that you are there when you are.'

He said softly, 'All the time I hope, dear girl. Ah, here is your . . . What is he, Rose?'

'Nothing,' she snapped and turned a welcoming smile on Percy Pride.

That young man gave her a casual hullo and a rather more polite 'Good morning, Sir' to Sybren who enquired innocently, 'Busy, Mr Pride?'

'Day off, Sir. Had a lazy morning, forgot I was taking Rose out actually!' He turned to her, missing Mr Werdmer ter Sane's contemptuous look. 'You didn't mind waiting, did you, Rose? There's plenty of time, we can have a snack at the British Museum and then spend the afternoon there.'

Mr Werdmer ter Sane uttered a choked sound which he turned into a cough.

'That sounds most interesting.' He gave Rose a limpid look. 'You'll enjoy that.' His smile was quite nasty; she had come to dread seeing it, especially just then; she would have liked to retire to some dark isolated spot and have a good cry, but only after hitting Sybren over the head with something really hard and doing the same for the wretched Percy.

Sybren, watching her, read her thoughts very accurately, she had that kind of a face, for him at any rate. She was in for a dull day, by the end of it she would probably not be on speaking terms with Percy. It served her right for being proud and stubborn and jumping to all the wrong conclusions. All the same he made a mental note to be around that evening, he didn't think that Percy was a young man to splash out on dinner unless he was getting something in return, an aspect which Rose, being Rose, had overlooked.

He said pleasantly, 'Well, enjoy yourselves, it's a splendid day.'

Which it was, only not a day to spend in a museum, thought Rose, going outside with Percy. They took the bus. He had a car, he explained, but it wasn't worth driving the short distance from the hospital and spending a fortune on parking fees. Rose, anxious to make the day a success, agreed and stood un-complainingly between a very stout woman with a shopping bag smelling of fish and a youth with a strange hair-do and a radio strapped to his belt. At least she heard the midday news.

When Percy had told Mr Werdmer ter Sane that they would have a snack, that was exactly what he had meant. Rose, eating beans on toast and making every mouthful tell, thought waspishly of mushrooms in cream sauce and lobster thermidor, though Sybren hadn't meant a word of it, and over their coffee listened with all the interest she could summon to Percy carrying on about his career. 'Of course I don't intend to be a paediatrician,' he told her. 'I'm not keen on kids; they're grubby and sick up. I shall specialise in cardiac surgery, there's a wide field and plenty of money there.'

'Is there?' Rose was a little vague; she never thought of surgery in terms of money although she was aware that surgeons for the most part were comfortably well off. 'So you'll go to one of the cardiac hospitals when you're finished at St Bride's?'

'Naturally, St Bride's is only a stop-gap until there is a vacancy.'

'But St Bride's does very important work—look at little Shirley—that was a marvellous piece of surgery Mr Werdmer ter Sane did—she'd be dead by now . . .'

He shrugged. 'She'll have one leg shorter than the other if she lives.'

'Of course she'll live,' said Rose indignantly, 'and there are such things as surgical shoes . . .'

'Well, don't let's bore on about work. If you're finished, shall we move into the museum?'

It appeared that Percy liked mummies. He knew a lot about them too; he lectured Rose at length about each specimen and she disliked every minute, trying not to look too closely at the remains he was so enthusiastic about, her thoughts turning more and more to lobster thermidor. Mercifully, he stopped at teatime and marched her along to the cafeteria for a cup of tea and a sponge cake which merely sopped up the tea and left her insides empty. It was over tea that Percy told her that he had the key to a friend's flat. 'We'll nip along there,' he told her, 'and have a drink—there's food in the fridge; no one will know if you don't get back to St Bride's—I suppose you're on in the morning; well, as long as we're back before breakfast . . .' He rambled on happily while she sat staring at him. Was this what Sadie had meant when she had said that he wasn't quite Rose's type? She said clearly, 'I think you've got it wrong. I've no intention of going to anyone's flat with you, Percy. Whatever gave you that idea?'

He lolled back in his chair, still very sure of himself. 'My dear girl, aren't you a bit out of date? Nowadays we live just as we like . . .'

'Yes, we do,' said Rose coldly, 'and I don't think we like the same sort of life.'

'My God, you're stuffy.' The sneer on his face quite spoilt his good looks.

Rose, wishing to be fair, considered this. 'Yes, I dare say I am,' she conceded. 'Thank you for a very pleasant afternoon, Percy.'

She picked up her shoulder bag from beside her chair, got up and walked away, looking quite composed and under the calm seething.

She was also hungry. On the bus going back to the hospital, she tried to decide what she would do with her evening. Sadie was on duty, her other friends were either on duty too, or had dates. Fish and chips, she told herself philosophically, and the new novel a little patient's grateful parent had presented to her a few days ago. Anything would be better than spending the evening, not the night, with Percy. She shuddered strongly at the very idea, descended from the bus and went briskly across the hospital's forecourt, watched by the patient Sybren.

He strolled towards her as she crossed the entrance ahead of him, blocking her path so that she was forced to stop. 'Had a good time?' he wanted to know blandly.

He really was the last straw. 'You again,' declared Rose in a regrettably shrill voice. 'I might have known. And if you've come to gloat, you can get on with it, but don't you dare stop me . . .'

The voice in which he uttered, 'Now, now,' would have soothed an ill-tempered baby in the throes of teething. 'You don't have to say a word. I just happened to be here,' he uttered the fib with a magnificent candour. 'If you could forget that you don't like me and have dinner with me? I dislike eating on my own.' He gave a fleeting thought to his solitary meals in his home and smiled very faintly. 'If you're not hungry we could cut out the lobster.'

She had meant to say no but her insides rumbled in the silence following his words and he added matter-of-factly, 'You're hungry too.'

She gave him one of her clear looks. 'Yes, I am. I'll come and thank you but only—only . . .'

'As ships that pass in the night? Oh, that's understood.' He turned her round smartly and made for the door.

'I'm not—I really ought . . .' She began and was silenced by his, 'You can do whatever you need to do while I'm seeing about a table.'

After that he had nothing to say; she sat in the comfort of the Rolls, her head empty of thoughts, in a dreamlike state from which she felt sure she would wake presently. But she didn't; Sybren parked the car and ushered her into the restaurant with a kindly, 'Off you go, I'll be here when you're ready.'

She spent ten minutes doing her face and her hair and wishing that she had been wearing something smart enough for her surroundings. The pink was all right, but she had worn it several times, he must think she hadn't anything else. Apparently he didn't for when she joined him he remarked, 'I like that dress better than any of the others you wear. Pink suits you.'

She thanked him shyly and followed the head waiter to a table by a window, nicely secluded.

'Well, now shall we have champagne cocktails while we decide what we'll eat? His manner was just right, the old friend taking out another old friend he'd accidently met. For the whole of their delicious meal he made no mention of the hospital, or Percy Pride or Holland for that matter. He seemed to have an inexhaustible fund of small talk which needed little or no reply on her part. As they went from mushrooms to lobster and from lobster to a magnificent concoction of ice cream, chocolate and whipped cream crowned with raspberries, Rose unwound. Sybren, filling her glass with the excellent champagne he had ordered, lifted a finger for coffee and sat back while their plates were taken away and it was brought. Only then did he ask, 'Do you want to tell me about it, Rose? Regard me as a sympathetic aunt if you wish, or one of your friends at St Bride's. It doesn't matter that you don't like me; I promise you I'll forget about it at once. You see if you bottle it up it will grow out of all proportion and you'll rake it up,' and when she didn't speak, 'what did you have for lunch? Beans on toast?'

She laughed then. 'Yes, and a cup of coffee . . .'

'I've never liked beans since I ate them out of a tin when I was a scout.'

'You were a scout?' She looked so surprised that he laughed. 'It keeps little boys out of mischief. What part of the museum did you visit?'

'The mummies. I—I didn't much care for them and it seems so rude to stare at them when they've been dead for such a long time.'

'True. Young Pride is interested in them?'

'Oh yes!' She found herself smiling. 'He lectured me.' She sipped her coffee and didn't look at him. 'We had tea then and he—he told me that he had the key of a friend's flat . . .'

She glanced at him and somehow he wasn't Mr Werdmer ter Sane any more but someone she could talk to without feeling a fool. It was a facet of him she hadn't seen before although, loving him, she thought that she knew him very well. 'I should have thought of that, shouldn't I?' she ended.

He said gravely: 'I think that perhaps your friend Sadie would have, but you . . . no, Rose. You haven't had much experience of men, have you?'

The warm friendly feeling faded. She said woodenly, 'No, for obvious reasons.' She was suddenly cross because he had spoilt the evening. 'And you have no need to remind me—haven't I been told since I was a teenager that I was plain—homely was the word my stepmother used and she was so right—men don't make passes at homely girls, only when there's no one else available I suppose.' Her voice squeaked with temper. 'You should know that.'

She put down her cofee-cup and said like a small child, 'Thank you for my dinner, I'd like to go back now.'

Mr Werdmer ter Sane hadn't said a word; he paid the bill, accompanied her from the restaurant, saw her into the car and drove her back to St Bride's, still without speaking. Only as he opened the door for her did he say, 'Good night, Rose—goodbye perhaps?' He touched her cheek with a gentle finger and got back into the car and drove away.

CHAPTER EIGHT

LYING in bed, trying to get to sleep, Rose admitted that she had been silly as well as rude; no wonder Sybren hadn't spoken to her on their way back from the restaurant. She was going to have to apologise to him; he would probably be on the ward in the morning. She shut her eyes and drifted into an uneasy sleep.

Sister was back on duty in the morning which left Rose free to attend to Shirley who despite the antibiotic was slightly feverish and pretty peevish. The registrar came during the morning, attended by a sulky Percy, who avoided Rose's eye and, most unusual for him, had nothing to say for himself. The registrar examined Shirley without haste, his face expressionless. He was worried, Rose guessed, and to tell the truth she was worried herself; the child wasn't making progress and she had been doing so well.

'We'll keep her on the antibiotic for another twenty-four hours, Rose,' the registrar told her. 'If her temperature isn't coming down by then, we'll have to think again. Mr Werdmer ter Sane went back this morning but he'll come over again if we're worried; he didn't want Mr Cesswell's holiday interrupted, he's not due back until Sunday.'

He went away and when she had settled Shirley she went into the ward to get started on the treatments and dressings. It was a day when things went wrong; nothing important, just small irritating things; notes mislaid, a child who should have gone home, delayed, not enough sheets back from the laundry, the dispensary querying Percy Pride's prescriptions; and quite rightly too for he wrote very small and with flourishes which could be taken for anything. Rose went off duty that evening feeling that it had been a day of twice its usual length.

The rest of the week was much the same, too, although she was ready to admit to herself that she was partly to blame; try as she would, she found it quite impossible to stop thinking about Sybren, largely because she had no idea if she would ever see him again. Shirley seemed to get better although she wasn't making the progress she should and she knew that the registrar was worried about her although there was nothing he could put his finger on. Her small chest had improved and yet she was listless and very peevish, not bothering when her mother came to sit with her for hours at a stretch. Rose, going off-duty on Friday evening for the weekend, was vaguely worried about the child; the operation had been a success, there was no doubt of that, and yet Shirley wasn't doing as well as she should. Sister Cummins, drinking her coffee with Rose on the Friday, voiced her unease. 'I shall be glad when Mr Cresswell is back on Sunday; I only wish we could have got hold of Mr Werdmer ter Sane but Mr Farrell tells me he had to go to Munich on some urgent case and can't get here before tomorrow. Still I dare say the three of them will put their heads together. You're pale, Rose, it's a good thing you have this weekend off.'

Rose didn't agree with her; she was going to miss seeing Sybren; he would be gone by the time she got back at midday on Monday. Well, it was her own fault; he had asked to be forgiven. She wondered why; it surely couldn't make much difference to him, she had been—what had he said? A ship which passed in the night.

When she got to her aunt's cottage that lady eyed her severely. 'Rose, what have you been doing with yourself? You're washed out, no colour at all, all eyes and much too thin.'

Rose said with a false cheerfulness, 'Well, that's a good thing, I'm too fat, you know.'

'Rubbish, child. Maggie, we'll have a bottle of that port the vicar gave me for Christmas, and you, Rose, sit down and eat your supper. I know it's late and you are tired, but no one ever slept on an empty stomach.'

It was soothing to be taken so firmly in hand with her aunt on one side plying her with port and Maggie urging second helpings and when she was told to go to bed with the hot milk Maggie had put into her hand, she went willingly enough and presently laid her head on her pillow and went instantly to sleep.

She was up early, feeling marvellous, drinking a cup of tea with Maggie in the kitchen and then taking Shep for a walk before breakfast. And over that meal Aunt Millicent observed that there was really nothing much to do but if she liked to accompany her to the church to do the flowers she was more than welcome.

The church was small and old and cool and the vicar came along while they were arranging their vases and had a long, rather prosy chat, a pleasant hotchpotch of local news, the amount of honey he was getting from his hives, old Mrs James's poor health and the forthcoming Sunday School treat. Rose found it all very soothing.

'And you, Rose?' he wanted to know. 'How is life treating you? You are able to enjoy your leisure, I hope; your work is hard but worthwhile and nurses deserve their pleasure even more than the rest of us.'

She assured him that yes, life was splendid and there was always something to do when she was off duty and she had so many friends . . .

Aunt Millicent, arranging a massive bouquet for the font, for there was a christening on Sunday, glanced at her niece. From the look of the girl, she mused, none of that was true. Telling fibs, in church too, and to the vicar but the dear child was unhappy about something. Aunt Millicent thought privately that she would like to meet this Dutch surgeon Rose was so careful never to mention. Maggie, an elderly spinster and with a romantic heart, had declared that little Rose was in love and Aunt Millicent had a shrewd suspicion that she might be right.

She bore Rose back to the cottage presently to eat a substantial lunch and then take Shep for his afternoon walk. 'For I am quite exhausted,' said Aunt Millicent, who had never been exhausted in her life but held the view that there was nothing like a good walk in the open air to ease one's feelings.

As for Rose, she walked for miles until even Shep slowed his steps and when she got back to the cottage she looked all the better for it with colour in her cheeks and a readier smile. She was given sherry, told to tidy herself for her supper and plied with good wholesome food before sitting down to a game of bezique with her aunt and then being packed off to bed with Maggie trotting up the stairs presently to see that she drank her milk. The two old ladies' sensible kindness did much to restore Rose's equanimity; a Sunday spent as they always were at the cottage: church, lunch, a lazy afternoon in the garden with tea under the trees edging the lawn and one of Maggie's delicious cold suppers to round off the day, more or less completed the cure. At least it had made her see that life had to go on whether she loved Sybren or not and she would have to make the best of it. She slept dreamlessly and went back to London in the morning. It was obvious that things weren't quite right when she went on duty after her early dinner. Sister Cummins pounced on her at once.

'Good, you're back. My goodness, what a weekend and you not here. Mr Werdmer ter Sane has just gone; Mr Cresswell's still in the hospital if we want him. Shirley took a turn for the worse yesterday, thank heaven both men came back together; she's on a life support machine—fat embolism—you were worried about her chest, remember? They did a tracheostomy last night—there's respiratory failure. Let's hope there's no brain damage. She's unconscious, of course. She's being treated by hypothermia. I've been looking after her and they sent a staff nurse to manage the ward; now you're back, take her over, will you?'

Sister Cummins was tired and, unlike her, ruffled. She allowed Rose to sit her down at her desk and fetch her a tray of tea from the kitchen.

'Who's with Shirley?' she asked, sugaring her tea lavishly and opening a tin of biscuits.

'Staff Nurse White from the medical side—she's quite good, but she's not dealt with a fat embolism before . . .'

'And in the ward?'

'The two part-timers and the junior student nurse; they can cope.'

'Then Sister, would you agree to going off duty for a few hours? If Doris White could go into the Ward, I'll see to Shirley. Mr Farrell's on duty, isn't he? And he can get hold of Mr Cresswell.' She couldn't stop herself asking, 'Is Mr Werdmer ter Sane coming back?'

'I don't know. He flew over yesterday afternoon; he was here until a short while ago. He and Mr Cresswell think there's just a chance; she's holding her own.' Sister Cummins was reviving rapidly under the influence of strong tea. 'Everything was going so well too, and it's a bit late in the day for a fat embolism, I mean, no one expected it after the first few days.' She poured another cup of tea. 'Now I'll give you a report and take your advice and have an hour or two off. You're on until the night staff come, aren't you?' She added belatedly, 'Did you have a good weekend?'

'Lovely, thanks, Sister.'

'You look better for it. I'll come back to give the report, shall I?' That will leave you free to see to Shirley before you go off-duty. Staff Nurse White can see to the ward—relieve each other for supper.'

It was a good thing that there were no other very ill children; all the same, there was more than enough to do and Shirley needed constant care. Rose sipped a cup of tea one of the nurses brought her and hardly noticed the time. When she got off-duty at last she was tired and hungry. Mr Cresswell had been in and so had Mr Farrell and Percy Pride had been with them, out of his depth, she suspected, although he looked as though he knew exactly what was going on. Her last thoughts before she slept were a sure hope that she would never be in a tight corner with him.

She was on all day for the next day or two; she had breakfast with the other girls and was on duty by half past seven, the long day stretching ahead of her but not minding that; it was a good thing to have something to think about, something urgent enough to dispel Sybren from her mind.

It was mid-afternoon with only another couple of hours before she could go off-duty when he came into the ward. He nooded briefly at her, said, 'Let someone know I'm here, will you?' and went to look at Shirley.

Mr Farrell came almost immediately followed by Percy, and Mr Werder ter Sane asked, 'Where is Sister Cummins?'

'Off-duty, Sir,' said Rose and when he frowned a little went indignantly pink although she asked reasonably enough, 'Would you like Staff Nurse White here, Sir? She's been nursing Shirley.' She gave him a calm look, hiding her hurt feelings. He didn't want her on the case any more; well, that was all right by her. She met his cold eyes without a blink. How puzzling it was that she could love him so wholeheartedly and find him such a very tiresome man.

'That won't be necessary, Staff Nurse. Shall we have the charts?'

He was there quite some time, discussing what was best to be done, and presently Mr Cresswell arrived and they stood around muttering and murmuring to each other, while Percy hovered on their perimeter and Rose sensibly got on with her observations, checked her tubes and paraphernalia, taking no notice of the learned gentlemen and their deliberations. They gathered round the child presently and Mr Werdmer ter Sane said, 'If you will continue the treatment, Staff Nurse, and notify Mr Farrell of any change.' He looked at Mr Cresswell who nodded agreement and who then said surprisingly, 'Good work, Rose, keep it up.'

But Sybren said nothing, merely nodded even more briskly than before and walked away with Mr Cresswell, leaving Mr Farrell to give her a friendly pat on the shoulder as he followed them. Percy would have spoken to her but she said rather crossly, 'I'm busy—do you mind?' and went back to her dials and tubes.

She didn't see Sybren again, although he was in and out for the next day or so, always when she was off-duty or at a meal. Little Shirley began to show signs of recovery; a slow recovery but steady. Now it was a question of waiting to see if she had suffered any brain damage and Rose, watching the small signs of returning consciousness, prayed that that had been avoided. Shirley was still on her life-support machine and would be for another few days, after that they could be optimistic.

The weather was unusually warm and Rose longed to be at her aunt's cottage out in the fresh air, taking Shep for his stately walk, doing a little undemanding gardening. She did go for a brief walk each evening with whoever was off-duty with her, but there was only the nearby park and besides the streets round the hospital were crowded by various processions of people chanting for or against something. Usually they didn't come on to the streets until the early evening, but as she went about her work in the early afternoon she could hear a good deal of shouting in the distance. Sister Cummins, coming in to take a look at Shirley before she went off duty, remarked upon it. 'I'll be glad to get away from the din for the evening,' she observed, 'I'm off to Maidenhead. See you in the morning. There is nothing new since I went over the report with you.'

Staff Nurse White was in the ward with two student nurses and since half the children were convalescent she would be able to cope easily. Rose began to bed-bath Shirley, still unconscious but restless. She was just finishing when one of the student nurses came into the room to tell her that Percy Pride was in the ward.

'Staff thought you'd like to know,' she explained. 'He's just pottering around.'

Rose nodded. 'He would, leave the door open, will you? Have the children had their teas? Will you ask Rene if she'll make a pot of tea for Staff and me? You two go to tea at four o'clock, will you?'

She was alone again, bending over Shirley when the world seemed to explode around her, a thunder of sound which rumbled and grumbled to a never-ending crashing of brickwork and masonry and tinkling glass.

Rose wanted to scream, as it was she was terribly afraid and trembling so much that she had to put down the thermometer she was holding, but the discipline of years of training took over; the ventilator, not surprisingly, had come to a halt; she started the manual emergency and switched on the oxygen from the cylinder, aware that Doris, her face as white as her own and shaking just as badly, was at her elbow. 'The windows are blown out, thank God the glass went outside, the floor's sagging . . .'

'Three of you—four with Percy, if the stairs are safe get the children down to the next floor—stay in the ward, get a nurse on the landing and another at the bottom of the stairs—make a chain; get Percy to help.'

'But you? I'll send Percy here as soon as the children are safe.'

'I'm all right for the moment, and there's the door over there.' She nodded towards a small door at the back of the room which led to a narrow passage, relic of the earlier days of St Bride's and seldom used. 'Hurry, Doris.'

There was noise all around, but not very close, people shouting, ambulances wailing, running feet. Rose, feeling that she was in the middle of a particularly nasty dream, worked away at her machine and hoped for the best. Someone would come soon and if she gave way to panic both she and Shirley would come to grief.

She could hear frenzied activity in the ward and then silence before Doris called, 'We're empty Rose, and Percy's coming.'

But before he came there was a slow shudder as the outside wall of the ward swayed slowly outward and disappeared. There was still the width of the ward between Shirley's room, and a good stout wall besides, although the door was hanging on its hinges. Rose made a small sound which might have been a sob and then pulled herself together again. They would have to risk making a run for it once Percy came back. They would go through the ward and down the stairs; he could carry the child while she pumped; it would be touch and go but better than staying where they were.

He came in slowly, almost reluctantly, his face pale, 'The stairs,' he said hoarsely, 'they've just fallen to bits, we'll never get out that way.'

'Then we'll go along the passage: it's narrow and it'll take twice as long but we're sure to find help. You warned someone we're here?'

He looked at her and she saw that he wasn't listening. She said it all again, fear making her shrill, and this time he said, 'Help, no I didn't. We'll never get away,' he repeated.

She had a blanket ready. 'We'll have to manage without the oxygen—pick her up carefully and don't go too fast or I'll never be able to keep up,' she said bracingly, more to reassure herself than him. 'There's sure to be someone . . .'

In the distance someone yelled 'Fire!' and she froze. 'Get a move on, Percy,' she managed from a shaking mouth and opened out the blanket.

'I'll get help.' He had turned and rushed out through the door before she could speak. Her first frantic attempt to shout after him came out as a very small squeak, the second was an ear-splitting yell, unfortunately drowned by the urgent sirens of approaching fire engines. She couldn't believe that he had gone away and left them; he knew, even better than she, that Shirley needed two people to get her to safety. She shouted again still hopeful that he had gone for help and would come back at any moment, but there was no reply, only ominous creaks and groans from the building and the faintest whiff of smoke.

Something would have to be done; anything was better than staying there waiting for the roof to fall in or to be enveloped in flames. She remembered Doris, then, she would have told someone; Rose took fresh heart, snatched up some towels in her free hand, planning to wet them in the wash basin. She would disconnect Shirley, go through the door into the passage and go as fast as she could until she reached the small stairs at its end. They opened into, for some reason which she had never bothered about, one of the underground passages which honeycombed the hospital's foundations. There were several doors leading into the courtyard around the building, once there they could get Shirley on to a portable ventilator. Even as she planned she knew that the chances of the child surviving were small. She filled her lungs and gave a great shout.

This time she was answered. 'All right, I'm not deaf,' said Mr Werdmer ter Sane, bending his large person so that he could get through the door.

Sybren had been driving towards St Bride's when the

bomb exploded, too far off to suffer any injury but near enough to the hospital to have a good idea that it would have been caught in the blast. He parked his car and shouldered his way through the still running crowds. The entrance was damaged but still standing, one wing more or less undamaged excepting blown-out windows, but the surgical wing had received a good share of the bomb's force, and Sister Cummins' ward was exposed to the outside world although there was no sign of life there. He had crossed the entrance hall already crowded with patients and nurses and house doctors organising them into a semblance of order when he saw Staff Nurse White. He put out an arm and stopped her. 'Rose, where is she?' he wanted to know.

'Still with Shirley; at least I asked Percy Pride to go back and help her; they ought to be here.' She looked round helplessly. 'He said he'd see to everything so I haven't told anyone—I had the ward to see to.'

He said soothingly because she was on the verge of tears, 'Of course—don't worry—I'll see if I can find them.'

There was a good deal of rubble blocking his way and before he reached the stairs outside the ward he could see that it was a hopeless task to get up them. He went back the way he had come, the smell of smoke strong in his nostrils. There would be another way up to the ward; he would have to lose precious minutes looking for it.

There was no need, a door along the passage in front of him burst open and Percy came hurtling towards him. 'We must get out,' he pushed Sybren's arm away, 'the place is on fire.'

'Where is Rose?' Sybren's voice expected an answer, fire or no fire.

'With Shirley . . .'

'And you left them to roast alive?' Mr Werdmer ter Sane uttered strong language in his own tongue. 'You will get doctors or porters or police—anyone, a trolley, oxygen and a portable ventilator and you will bring them to this door at once and wait here'. He added grimly, 'If you do not, I personally shall break every bone in your body.'

He didn't wait to see how Percy reacted but tore through the door, closing it behind him. The stairs faced him; he went up them at a surprising speed considering how heavily built he was. The narrow passage at the top seemed endless and the smell of smoke was stronger. He saw the door at its end and opened it with a grunt of relief.

Rose stared at him from a pale frightened face, still working away at the ventilator. She opened her mouth to speak but no sound came which was a good thing. From the look on his face he was in no mood to stand any female nonsense. He was disconnecting Shirley from the useless machine and wrapping her in the blanket. 'Work the ventilator and keep close,' he bade Rose and without more ado he made for the door. It was a tight squeeze going along the passage and even worse on the stairs. Rose performed miracles of balance, her heart in her mouth, her arms aching beyond belief, her eyes stinging from the smoke eddying lazily around them. If she had had any breath left she would have whooped with joy when they reached the door. Mr Werdmer ter Sane gave it a vicious kick and it flew open and they burst through it untidily into instant activity. Percy Pride, doubtless anxious about his bones, had assembled all that Sybren had told him to get. Shirley, connected to oxygen and the ventilator and warmly wrapped, was laid on a trolley and borne away with Mr Werdmer ter Sane in charge and Percy, anxious to make amends, hovering. There were quite a few people in the procession and no one had noticed that Rose wasn't with them.

She watched them go, leaning against the broken door. She felt a little light-headed but sensible enough to reason that it was natural enough for them all to concentrate on Shirley, and probably the burly policeman who was giving a hand had thought she was just being curious when he had moved her gently aside from the trolley and told her to get out of the way. She would have to make her own way to the entrance hall and find Doris and the rest of the children.

Shirley was being taken to the undamaged wing, being hastily organised to take as many children as possible. Mr Cresswell was already there and he and Sybren bent over Shirley, assessing the damage. She was still alive. 'And probably none the worse for it,' said Mr Cresswell with satisfaction. 'How long has she been off the life-support machine?'

'Rose?' Sybren looked around when she didn't answer. 'Where's Rose?' He looked again. 'Did anyone see her? She came through the door with me.'

He didn't wait for an answer but turned and went back the way they had come and found her still leaning against the door. 'What on earth are you hanging round here for?' He sounded so angry that she blinked at him. He couldn't even rescue her without getting cross about it, she thought wearily. 'I'm going to find Staff Nurse White,' she said in a voice quite devoid of expression. She added idiotically, 'I'm sorry we were such a nuisance, Sir.'

She had whipped past him and sped around the

corner towards the entrance hall before he could stop her.

It took a little while to find Doris; the hall was full of firemen, ambulance men, doctors and nurses all intent on getting the children back into some sort of shelter as quickly as possible. Some were being taken by ambulance to neighbouring hospitals, the really ill ones were being bedded down in the far wing, which was happily undamaged.

'There you are, Rose—I've been so worried about you—Percy got you out? How is Shirley?' She eyed Rose's face. 'Are you all right? You're a kind of pea green . . .'

'I'm fine. Are all the children still here?'

'Yes—I'm on my way there just now. I came back to report to Casualty Sister, she's doing all the checking. Come with me—we've got the little ward at the end— you know the one? It's too small but we'll have to manage. I say, you were a brick to stay, Rose . . .' Staff Nurse White, who wasn't a talkative girl, said shyly, 'I wouldn't have dared—I was scared stiff . . .'

'So was I, if there'd been anyone there to hear I'd have screamed.'

'But Percy?'

'Not Percy—Mr Werdmer ter Sane.'

Doris White paused in her headlong rush through the crowds. 'Him? He rescued you? Where was Percy?' She gulped, 'Rose, he told me he was going back for you.'

'He changed his mind. At least he did get to us, but he went away again. But don't let on . . .'

The ward they entered was crowded with cots, beds, nurses and doctors with a porter or two thrown in. The babies were all at one end, bawling with rage at being disturbed, to everyone's relief. The toddlers were two to a bed at the moment, apparently unaware that anything untoward was afoot; Shirley had a bed to herself with one nurse working the ventilator and another one controlling the flow of oxygen. Mr Cresswell was there, so was Sybren; they looked at her as she and Doris went across the ward, Mr Cresswell with a warm welcoming smile tinged with faint alarm at Rose's unfortunate colour; Sybren with a cold eye which apparently hadn't noticed.

All the same he was the one to catch her as she crumpled up in an untidy heap. With a muttered word to Mr Cresswell he strode out of the ward, across the back of the still crowded entrance and kicked open the door of the nurses' home.

There were a lot of people there too, going to and fro in a purposeful manner. He stopped a distracted woman with a fierce hair-do and a blue overall. 'Which room is Staff Nurse Comely's?' he barked at her.

She put an agitated hand on her substantial bosom. 'You can't come in here . . .'

'I can and I will, which room?'

'I'm the warden . . .'

Mr Werdmer ter Sane, not naturally a patient man, was losing his temper now. 'I don't give a damn what you are. The number?'

She told him, gobbling with annoyance.

'And why don't you get into the hospital and give a hand instead of wringing your hands here?' he demanded and took the stairs two at a time.

It was a good thing he was a large strong man; Rose wasn't heavy but she had a room on the second floor. By the time he reached her door he was breathing rather faster than usual.

He laid Rose gently upon her bed, took off her cap,

covered her with a blanket and felt her pulse. It was quite satisfactory; he fetched a glass of water from the wash basin and sat down on the side of the bed and studied her. There was nothing faintly glamorous about her; her hair was in a deplorable state, hanging in wisps around her pale face. Her apron had been dragged askew and she had laddered her tights and there was a cut on one arm where she had caught it on some wreckage on their way to safety. He bent and kissed her very gently and waited patiently until she opened her eyes a few minutes later.

'Where . . .' she began and stopped. Heroines in novels always asked where they were when they had fainted. Instead she said, 'I'm sorry I fainted. So silly.'

'So sensible. Nature's way of putting you out of action so that you can recoup your strength.' He sounded as dry as one of her text books.

She sat up, the pea green had given way, thankfully, to pallor, and she drank the water he was offering. 'I'm quite all right, thank you,' she told him in a voice which belied her wan appearance. 'I'm sure you want to get back.'

'How long were you there alone?' he asked.

'Oh, not long. I'm not sure . . .' She forced her voice to it's usual matter-of-fact calm. 'One doesn't notice time when one is busy.'

'Or when one is scared out of one's wits,' he commented blandly. 'You're a very brave girl, Rose. You could have killed Shirley if you'd panicked and you could both have been killed there.'

'You came . . .'

'Yes.' He got up. 'I'm going to find someone to bring you a hot drink and you are to lie there warm and quiet for at least half an hour, after that you may return to duty. Those are doctor's orders.'

He went very quietly and she put her head back on the pillow, glad to rest it. Ten minutes later one of the home sisters came in with a tea tray. 'I had no idea,' she began comfortably, 'Mr Werdmer ter Sane came looking for me and told me. You poor child, what a frightful experience, left alone like that. You were doing your duty, of course, but I can think of any number who wouldn't have stuck their necks out when there was a chance of getting killed or burnt to a crisp.'

She put the tray down and poured the tea out and then poured something into it.

'What's that?' asked Rose.

'Whisky, my dear. Mr Werdmer ter Sane ordered it for you. Drink it up, there's a good girl.'

Rose had swung her legs over the bed. 'I must get back—there'll be such a lot to do,' she began.

'Bound to be.' Home Sister was unflappable. 'I popped over a little while ago to give a hand.' She chuckled. 'He didn't think much of our warden, I might have known she'd go to pieces—still that's neither here nor there. They've got everyone out, no one killed in the hospital, thank heaven, but several poor souls who were out in the street; quite a few children hurt, but not badly—your wing got the full blast, most of the centre and the other wing are more or less intact—and the nurses' home, of course. They have transferred the children who've been hurt and two of the student nurses, one of the porters and a domestic worker. I hear almost all the equipment has been damaged though.'

She re-filled Rose's cup, stood over her while she drank it and picked up the tray.

'I'm going back on duty, Sister.'

'Yes, dear. Put on another apron first and do your hair, you look more like yourself again now.'

Ten minutes later Rose went back into the hospital. There still seemed to be a great deal of confusion but the entrance hall was emptying fast although there were several men there with cameras. She hardly noticed them but slipped back into the ward, had a word with Doris and went to look at Shirley. The child actually looked better; she was checking things with the nurse looking after her when Mr Cresswell joined her.

'Feeling better?' He gave her a kind smile. 'A nasty experience, Rose, but I—we are all proud of you, it takes pluck to be brave when there's no one there to see. Mr Werdmer ter Sane is in theatre, checking the damage; we decided that you ought to go off-duty until tomorrow but we knew that you wouldn't take any notice of anything that we said.' He went on briskly, 'Now let's see who we've got left here—I've sent two of the babies over to Margaret's, they've got respiratory failure and they'll do better over there; they can come back when we are straight.'

After that things fell slowly into place. The hospital was full of firemen and police and television cameras but work went on in the wards wherever possible. Rose gathered her team around her and gave the children their suppers and their medicine, rearranged the cots and beds, sent nurses to their supper in turn, conducted the senior nursing officer round her small patients, did another round with the registrar who had been off duty and had just arrived back, and then found some paper and wrote the report. The Kardex was gone in the ruins; a new one would have to be made out tomorrow, in the meanwhile she made a quick resumé of the day's happenings ready for the night staff, most of whom were already on duty anyway.

It was a boon and a blessing when the electricians managed to get the electricity going again and the reserve ventilator could be brought in and fixed up. Rose sent the student nurse who had been looking after Shirley off-duty, conferred with Doris White and did a final round of the sleeping children. 'You go to supper,' she told Doris, 'and take everyone with you, and ask someone to save me some food, will you? I'll be along as soon as the night people have settled in.'

Which took rather more time than she had thought; it was long after the usual hour when she left the ward and she was now so tired she loitered along the passage, stumbling a little over the hoses still lying around, not looking where she was going. She stumbled over Mr Werdmer ter Sane's large feet too, which brought her to a sudden halt.

'Oh, sorry, Sir.' She looked at him with tired eyes, and her gentle mouth drooped at his curt, 'You should be in bed. What are you doing traipsing around?'

'I'm going to my supper,' she told him with dignity. 'Good night, Sir.'

He put his hands on her shoulders, pinning her gently to the spot.

'Oh, Rose, what has happened to us? I thought we had become friends—more than friends. But you don't trust me, do you?'

'Does it matter? And I did trust you until Mies told me.' She wriggled under his hands. 'Oh, does it matter?' she asked again. 'I'm so tired.'

He let her go then. 'Of course. How thoughtless I am. Good night, Rose and sleep well.'

He had gone. She went to the canteen and ate what was on her plate and went to bed. She wanted to cry but she was too tired.

CHAPTER NINE

THE next few days went by in a well ordered chaos; it was surprising how swiftly the great piles of debris round the hospital and in the streets around it were cleared away. An army of workmen moved in, mending doors and windows, hanging huge tarpaulins over gaping walls as in the meantime the hospital fell into its routine, or something approximating to it. At least the little patients suffered no discomforts although there was a certain amount of improvisation with equipment and there was, for a day or two, a shortage of crockery and everything which everyone had tended to take for granted as being to hand when needed. But on the whole, they managed very well; all the small tiffs which occurred between the various wards and departments were forgotten, at least for the time being. The laundry supplied the linen to the wards without complaint, even allowed extra; the dispensary forbore from wasting the ward sister's time by querying entries in the dispensary book and there was an unending supply of egg and chips and soup in the canteen.

Rose went about her work, outwardly her usual matter-of-fact self, while inwardly she was as miserable as she had ever been in her whole life. If this is being in love, she told herself fiercely, then the quicker I forget about it the better. Mr Werdmer ter Sane had come twice during the week and on both occasions she had been off-duty. Anyone would think, she mused bitterly, that he had looked in the off-duty book so that he wouldn't have to meet me.

Which was exactly what he had done.

Percy had avoided her but she had hardly noticed that, in fact she didn't think about him at all. She wanted to forget those awful moments when she had been alone with Shirley and he was all part and parcel of them. She would never forget how she had felt when she had heard Sybren's voice, calm and unhurried, and she supposed that she never would.

The ward settled down; Sister Cummins, still brooding over the fact that she hadn't been there when she would have been most useful, had the ward organised by now even though it wasn't entirely to her liking, and Shirley, to everyone's delight and surprise, regained consciousness and began to pick up once more.

Towards the end of the week Rose encountered Percy Pride as she was on the way to the path. lab. He had been avoiding her and she hadn't minded; he had behaved shamefully and he must be feeling awkward about it, besides Sadie had told her that he had been on the carpet and advised to transfer to the convalescent home in Surrey run by St Bride's.

But if she had expected an apology from him she was to be mistaken. He stopped in front of her and said sourly: 'So—how is our little heroine getting on? Did you a good turn, didn't I, leaving you to hog the limelight?'

Rose gave him the kind of look she would have given something nasty under a stone; she wished that she could be like Sadie with a quick, telling retort on her tongue, but she couldn't think of anything to say.

Percy eyed her narrowly and when she didn't speak, 'Oh, well, it didn't do you much good with Mr

Werdmer ter Sane, did it? He's off home and I dare
say he'll forget about brave little Rose once he gets
there. You are not quite his cup of tea, are you?'

Rose, holding the path. lab. specimen in its dish
carefully in one hand, reached up and smacked his
cheek. It made a very satisfactory sound and was just
as good as the kind of caustic remark she was sure
Sadie would have made to him. She didn't wait to see
the results of her slap but walked on down the stairs
into the lab. If she was a little nervous about coming
out again in case he was lurking, she had no intention
of admitting it, even to herself.

Back on the ward she gave herself no time to
think about Sybren; he was going home, Percy had
said, and there was no point in him lying about that,
and probably once there, he would forget her.
Instead she kept her mind on her work, longing at
the same time for five o'clock to come so that she
might go off-duty. She had her two days off but she
wasn't going to Aunt Millicent's; she would potter
around until lunch time and then take herself up to
Regent Street and do some window-shopping and
there was bound to be someone off-duty on her
second day; they could go to Kew Gardens or take
rolls and cheese into Regent's Park. She tackled
Shirley's small wants with zest and not long after
five o'clock she went off-duty.

She was almost at the bottom of the big staircase
leading to the entrance hall when she saw Sybren
standing talking to Mr Cresswell. She couldn't go
back; he was facing her and would have seen her.

As indeed he had; he said something to Mr
Cresswell and crossed to the stairs so that they came
face to face on the bottom step.

She searched his face and could find nothing

comforting in it. 'You're leaving—Percy told me.' She put out a hand. 'So I'll say goodbye . . .'

He ignored the hand and she dropped it to her side. 'You want it to be goodbye, Rose?'

She said in a rush, 'Yes, oh yes, and I do thank you for rescuing me and Shirley and I hope that you will be very happy . . .'

He lifted his eyebrows at that. 'Happy, should I be?'

'Well, yes.' She wished that she could say all the right things, Sadie would have known; made some witty observations about being married and turned everything into a joke, something which she was quite unable to do.

'I'm glad about Shirley and you must be delighted. When she is grown up she'll think of you with gratitude.'

'And you, Rose; you're already grown up, how do you think of me?'

The warm colour washed over her face but she didn't look away.

'I shall think of you as a very eminent surgeon, Sir.'

'You flatter me. Goodbye, Rose.' He stood on one side and after a moment's hesitation she went past him, across the hall and through the door at the back which would take her to the nurses' home.

She went very fast, trying to run away from her unhappiness. Before she reached her room she had already made up her mind to go to Aunt Millicent. If she hurried she could get a train; the local bus would have left, but just for once she would be extravagant and get a taxi. She hurled things into an overnight bag, tore out of her uniform, showered and dressed, tied her hair back with very little thought as to her appearance, left a message for Sadie and nipped smartly to the hospital entrance, remembering to peer cautiously out into the forecourt first in case Sybren's car was still there. It wasn't. She gulped back the ridiculous hope and went to catch a taxi to the station.

She caught the train with seconds to spare and at the other end was lucky enough to find the vicar's sister, only too glad to share a taxi with her. Aunt Millicent's cottage looked cosy and welcoming under the summer evening sky; Rose flew down the path and opened the door, calling 'It's me, Rose,' and when Aunt Millicent poked her austere head round the sitting-room door, she dropped her bag and hugged that lady quite ruthlessly, fighting a great desire to burst into tears.

Aunt Millicent took a lightning glance at her niece's face and said heartily, 'Well, what a lovely surprise. I was only saying to Maggie this very evening how nice it would be if you were here for a day or two.'

She frowned fiercely at Maggie, who had come hurrying from the kitchen, and that lady on the point of saying something quite different agreed instantly and loudly. 'And there's a lovely little raised pie just waiting to be eaten,' she pointed out. 'Just you put that bag in your room and I'll get a tray.'

'And a glass of wine, I think,' declared her aunt, 'and if you're not too tired we long to hear about that awful bomb. I had such a splendid letter from your principal nursing officer and a charming one from Mr Werdmer ter Sane.'

Rose, on her way upstairs, whizzed round. 'He wrote? To you? what about?'

'Telling us what had happened and saying that your courage had saved a child's life. He wrote that you were a splendid nurse with a great sense of duty.'

Rose said, 'Oh, did he?' in a hollow voice. That was the sort of thing one could say about anyone; someone

one didn't like overmuch or someone to whom one was quite indifferent. She went upstairs to her pretty room and sat down on the bed and pulled herself together. Presently she went down again and ate the raised pie and drank the wine and with the two elderly ladies on either side of her gave them a tidied-up version of the bombing. After that she was urged to go to her bed with the promise of a nice day on the morrow, doing nothing. She kissed the two kind faces, drank the milk with Maggie standing over her, and went upstairs. She was sure that she wouldn't sleep and she had a lot to think about but the country silence was soothing and the gentle murmur of voices from downstairs acted far more efficiently than a sleeping pill. She slept.

Mr Werdmer ter Sane had left the outskirts of London behind him and was well on the way to the ferry which would take him back to Holland when he slowed the car at an exit, followed it down and round and started driving back to London again on the other side of the motorway. For a man accustomed to having his own way either by arrogance or charm, he found himself singularly helpless. Rose, unassuming, not even pretty, certainly tiresomely obtuse about some things, had wished him goodbye in a matter-of-fact manner which should have left him in no doubt as to her feelings, but her eyes, her lovely gentle eyes, mused Mr Werdmer ter Sane besottedly, had betrayed her. He was at a loss to know why she had taken such a dislike to him—after all they had gone through too. He put an elegant foot down hard, anxious to get back to St Bride's and find out.

The head porter was unable to help him. 'Saw Staff Nurse Comely go out this evening with me own eyes, Sir—'ad a bag with 'er too.'

Mr Werdmer ter Sane thought for a moment. 'Can you get hold of her friend? Sadie the name is—but that is all I know.'

Old Wilson said stolidly: 'Staff Nurse Gordon, Sir.' He had worked all his life at St Bride's but he couldn't remember a consultant ever wanting to speak to a staff nurse off-duty. 'She'll be over in the 'ome, being just off-duty as you might say.'

He applied himself to the phone. 'She'll be right over, Sir.'

Sadie came dancing through the door; no one looking at her would have guessed that not five minutes earlier she had been in her dressing-gown, drinking tea and about to wash her hair. Now the dressing-gown had been replaced by uniform and her hair was charmingly arranged under a snowy cap.

She said breathlessly, 'Hullo. It seems silly to call you Sir, but I suppose I must. I thought you'd forgotten me.'

'Impossible—although I must do my best—I hear you are to be married very shortly.' He smiled, at his most charming. 'Sadie, where's Rose?'

'Rose?' They had walked into the centre of the entrance hall where no one could overhear them. 'Is that why she went?'

'Where?'

'To her aunt's house at Ashby St Ledgers, that's in . . .'

'I know, I wrote to her aunt—Miss Curtis—it's somewhere near Daventry.'

'Four miles—go up the M1 and turn left. Too late to go now—they'll all be in bed. It's about seventy miles; that's nothing to you and your Rolls. I say, why do you want to see her, has something awful happened on the ward?'

He shook his head. 'No, nothing like that . . .'

'You're not going to tell me, are you?'

'No, Sadie, not now.'

'I shall ask Rose when she gets back on Sunday evening.'

'By all means. Thank you for your help. I hope you'll invite me to your wedding?'

'I say, will you come if I do? Rose is to be one of the bridesmaids, she is going to wear pink, she looks pretty in pink.'

'I have thought for some time that she looks pretty in anything.'

Old Wilson peering at them from his little box was shocked when she leaned up and kissed Mr Werdmer ter Sane's cheek. Really, what was the world coming to?

'Good luck,' said Sadie, 'Rose is a darling girl but very pig-headed.'

She whirled away blowing a kiss to Wilson as she passed.

Sybren left London after seven o'clock in the morning, breakfasted on the way and was tooling down Ashby St Ledgers brief main street before ten. He stopped once here to ask the way and presently stopped in the lane outside Aunt Millicent's cottage. He got out and stood a moment looking at it; the windows were all open as was the front door and at the side of the house, given over to the soft fruit, he could see Rose picking raspberries.

She turned round as he shut the gate behind him and started slowly up the path and then came across the grass towards her. His good morning was affable and gave her no clue at all as to why he was there, standing in front of her, an uncanny answer to her daydreams. She put the basket of fruit down carefully and said good morning in her turn and since the silence between them got rather too long for comfort she essayed a little light conversation.

'I thought you were going to Holland.'

'So did I, indeed I started my journey and changed my mind. I wanted to make quite sure that you had meant what you had said; that you had wanted it to be goodbye, Rose.'

She said very steadily, 'Yes, I did mean it. I'm sorry you came all this way . . .' She paused and being a truthful girl, added, 'No, I'm not sorry.'

He stared down at her. 'I believe that we are at cross purposes; and I think to get to the heart of the tangle I must go back to Holland.' He studied her face carefully. 'You really mean it, don't you, Rose?'

'Oh, yes. And if you don't mind I'd rather not talk about it.'

He nodded. 'Very well. We'll say goodbye for a second time. Do you not have a saying in English "Third time lucky"?'

She wasn't going to answer that. It would be so easy to tell him that she loved him; she had only to open her mouth, but there was Mies—such a suitable wife for a wealthy eminent surgeon—waiting for him to go back to her.

She asked politely, 'Have you had breakfast! I'm sure Aunt Millicent will be glad to give you something.'

'I had a meal on the way here. I'll be on my way.'

Not just yet, cried her heart, five minutes more—ten minutes more . . . Someone, somewhere heard her. Aunt Millicent poked her head out of the kitchen window and called in her no-nonsense voice, 'Rose, whoever that is bring him in for a cup of coffee.'

Aunt Millicent was well aware who it was; it was

Maggie who had seen him coming up the garden path and had rushed into the sitting-room to whisper the news, just as though anyone was near enough to overhear her.

'It's him,' she whispered excitedly, 'I'm sure of it, Miss Curtis—that Dutch surgeon Rose never talks about. Fine as fivepence and a splendid body of a man.'

So Miss Curtis had gone to peer from the kitchen window while Maggie got out the coffee-pot, and since Sybren accepted the offer at once there was nothing for it but to bring him into the house.

Aunt Millicent received him graciously, liking what she saw, and immediately embarked on a series of topics of an impersonal nature until he put his coffee-cup down, observing that he would have to leave if he were to catch the hovercraft from Dover; he didn't specify at what time it went and she didn't ask him, merely observed that she had been delighted to meet him and telling Rose to see him to his car. Rose, who had had almost nothing to say, obediently got to her feet, waited while first her aunt and then Maggie bade him goodbye, and then led the way down the hall and out of the front door. She could see the Rolls parked in the lane and wished it miles away so that Sybren couldn't get into it and drive out of her life. They reached the gate but when she put out a hand to open it he covered it with one of his own.

'I had my life planned,' he spoke quite quietly, 'unexciting but satisfactory enough and somehow it didn't concern me overmuch. And then we met.' He paused to stare down at her upturned face, and she said quickly, 'A flash in the pan, that's all it was—you don't need to explain; I don't want you to. It was kind of you to come but I've made up my mind.' She drew a deep breath and lied convincingly. 'I really don't want to see you again. Please go now.'

She steeled herself against another goodbye and was very surprised when he smiled as though he were genuinely amused about something. 'Sadie said that you were pig-headed.' He lifted the hand he had been covering with his and kissed it gently. '*Tot Ziens*, Rose.'

He got into his car, raised a casual hand in salute and drove away without a backward glance.

'He didn't kiss her,' worried Maggie from the sitting-room window. 'He's gone.'

'He'll be back,' said Miss Curtis. 'Oh, he'll be back, Maggie. He's not a man to come whining excuses, he's gone to find out what's got between them. I suspect that our little Rose has got the wrong end of the stick and is too pig-headed to let go.' She nodded in a pleased manner. 'He will make her a splendid husband.'

'I could do with another cup of coffee,' she went on in her usual forthright tone as Rose came wandering in through the door. 'We'll all have one and then I'll come and help with those raspberries, Rose, it's best to pick them before the heat of the day.

She led the way into the sitting-room and sat down by the coffee tray while Maggie went off to the kitchen to fetch some more coffee. 'A very pleasant man,' she commented casually, 'and one to be trusted I think. A good trait in a surgeon, not given to talking about himself either.'

Rose agreed, it was something she had only just realised herself.

Rose was kept pleasantly occupied for the rest of the day; to sit idle with nothing but one's sad thoughts was what Aunt Millicent described to herself as

unsuitable, so Rose picked fruit, bathed Shep, took
him for a walk with her aunt for company and then
after tea was taken to the village for a whist drive in
aid of one of Miss Curtis's worthy causes. She did
everything suggested to her in a docile manner, her
mind far away, going every inch of Sybren's journey
to his home. And on the way back home for supper,
she imagined him arriving at his lovely home on the
gracht; Mies would be there to welcome him, of
course, wearing something glamorous, and at the sight
of her he would forget all about a girl named Rose . . .
She fetched such a deep sigh that her aunt hurried
her indoors with the observation that she had tired herself
out. 'Supper,' decreed Miss Curtis firmly, 'and then
bed.'

Rose was indeed exhausted by her feelings, she slept
soundlessly almost immediately her head touched the
pillow, still thinking of Sybren.

Aunt Millicent kept her busy all the next day too,
doing all the undemanding small tasks which went
with village life, and the following morning she went
back to St Bride's, fortified by Aunt Millicent's
bracing therapy and an enormous cake baked by
Maggie, to be eaten with the bedtime cups of tea.

The ward was busy and Shirley, well on the way to
recovery now, was demanding: Rose was kept busy
which was a good thing; on duty at least she had little
time for her own thoughts, although that meant that
she saved them up for bedtime, lying awake thinking
of Sybren when she should have been asleep. At the
end of the week she had lost weight, and her brown eyes
looked enormous in a rather pale face. The houseman
who had replaced Percy Pride was forced to agree with
Percy's rather spiteful opinion that Rose was a
splendid nurse but nothing much to look at, although

he liked her. She would, in his opinion, make a chap a splendid sister.

Rose had days off at the end of the week, but she had decided against going to Aunt Millicent's, much as she would have liked to. She was aware that she wasn't the best of company, just as she was aware that her aunt and Maggie had bent over backwards to help her when Sybren went away. She spent her days off assiduously touring picture galleries and museums, seeing nothing of them, but they filled the days.

She had a letter from Christina during the next week, full of news and not a word about Sybren. And why should there be? He didn't belong to her world.

Another week dragged to its close and there was no sign of the warm summer weather abating. The idea of another two days spent inspecting museums was too much for Rose to face. She phoned Aunt Millicent to see if she might spend her free days with her and was left in no doubt as to her welcome. She had a free evening before her days off; she had already packed her overnight bag; she hurried off-duty, showered, changed into the pink dress because it gave her pale face some colour, and raced down to the entrance hall. She had cut things rather fine, she would have to get a taxi if she were to catch her train. She tore through the door, straight into Mr Werdmer ter Sane's substantial person.

It was more like walking into a tree trunk, surprise took her by the throat so that she was unable to utter a word, but Sybren, not surprised at all, steadied her with a hand on each shoulder and remarked,

'Ah, there you are,' taking her bag from a nerveless hand at the same time and steering her towards the Rolls parked within feet of them.

Rose found her voice, albeit a rather squeaky one. 'I've a train to catch—I'm going away, you can't . . .'

'Oh, but I can, my dearest love, in you get.'

He opened the car door and stuffed her ever so gently on to the seat and then went round the car's bonnet and got in beside her.

'This is so absurd,' Rose's voice was a shrill whisper. 'You simply cannot . . .! I don't understand . . .'

'We will have a little talk later.' His voice was soothing as though he were coaxing one of his small patients. He started the engine and tooled the car across the forecourt and out into the evening traffic. And he didn't say anything else at all until they were clear of the densest traffic and in the comparative peace and quiet of Hampstead, on the way to joining the M1.

'You thought that I was going to marry Mies,' observed Sybren in a conversational tone. 'If you could have asked me I would have told you that nothing was further from my mind. I am going to marry you, my dearest, I didn't realise it at first, but gradually you have taken over my life, my very heart— you and I are hopelessly entwined. I can't imagine living without you.'

'But Mies said . . .' began Rose. Her heart was thudding away to break her ribs but she tried to ignore it. 'She said that you were celebrating . . .'

'And you were a darling little fool to believe her. You are a very silly girl, Rose. You are also brave, honest, a delightful companion and my dream girl.' He sighed. 'And how I love you!'

Rose didn't speak: she sat savouring the words he had uttered, she had more or less digested them by the time they had reached the M1 and he allowed the Rolls to leap ahead.

She said shyly, 'I've been in love with you for a long time, Sybren, only I tried not to be because of Mies.'

He laid a hand over her clasped ones in her lap. 'It took me a little while to find Mies and discover exactly what she had told you.'

'How did you know that I was going to Aunt Millicent's this evening?'

'Sadie.'

She asked urgently, 'Sybren, do you really want to marry me?'

'Oh yes, my darling Rose, I really do, and if we were not on a motorway I would stop and underline that statement.'

With that she had to be content, for he didn't speak again until at last he turned the car off the motorway and made for Ashby St Ledgers. And then all he said was, 'What a very beautiful evening it is.' And Rose, who had hoped that he would call her his darling again, agreed rather coldly.

But she need not have worried. He stopped the car in the lane outside Aunt Millicent's gate and got out and came to help her out too, and at the gate he stopped. 'Darling girl.' He smiled and wrapped his arms around her and kissed her in a manner which left her with no doubts at all.

'I don't know anything about you,' said Rose weakly.

'Oh, yes you do. Haven't we worked together for weeks on end?'

'But your family? I mean, are you an orphan?'

'Lord no, sweetheart. Four sisters, all younger than I am, and a mother and father, all looking forward to meeting you.'

He bent to kiss her again and she kissed him back.

At the sitting-room window her aunt watched them

with deep satisfaction. 'I said he'd be back,' she told Maggie, peering out beside her.

'Lawks, Miss Curtis—he's kissing her.' She turned a beaming face to her companion. 'I'd best make up the spare-room bed; this time he'll be staying.'

ROMANCE

TUNE IN TO THE
VOICE OF ROMANCE . . .

DISCOVER LASTING LOVE.

True love is everlasting.

Rather like our Nostalgia Collection.

This delightful set of books gives a fascinating insight into the romances of the 30's, 40's and 50's.

Each decade had its own popular writers and we've chosen 3 of our favourites to take you back in time in their own distinctive style.

We've even re-printed the original covers, to create a real collector's item for lovers of romantic fiction.

We think you'll find that times may change, but true love simply improves as years go by.

Available from April 1986.

Price £4.75.